WELCOM

Jacky Fisher

In memory of Mel Harris

1959 – 2008

We miss you every day.

WELCOME HOME
Jacky Fisher

Patrick Harris

Who is Jacky Fisher and which side is he on?

Best wishes

NORTH DOWNS PRESS

First published in 2016 by North Downs Press
61 Kingshill Drive, Hoo St Werburgh, Rochester, Kent, ME3 9JW

Cover painting, *Jacky Fisher* © Hannah Collins

Distributed by Gardners Books, 1 Whittle Drive, Eastbourne, East Sussex, BN23 6QH
Tel: +44(0)1323 521555 | Fax: +44(0)1323 521666

British Library Cataloguing in Publication Data
A catalogue record for this book is available from the British Library

ISBN 978-0-9560829-1-6

Typeset by Amolibros, Milverton, Somerset
www.amolibros.co.uk
This book production has been managed by Amolibros
Printed and bound by T J International Ltd, Padstow, Cornwall, UK

The author was born in 1950 in Kent and still lives there. He was educated at the Harvey, Folkestone and Chatham Grammar Schools. He has now retired from the petro-chemical industry and is a widower. He has two grown-up children and is now a grandfather. This is his second novel, his first was a novella called *A Long Road Home*. He has written many short stories and poetry.

From the author:

Wisdom Hospice, Rochester, Kent

I support the Molly Wisdom hospice in Rochester Kent. I came to know of them when my late wife Mel Harris was admitted in the final days of her life. The hospice does fine work and as such I will donate one pound of every full price sale to them.

For individual donations please visit their website:
http://www.fowh.org.uk

Hannah Collins is a fine artist and illustrator working in London and South Wales. She graduated from Lancaster University in 2012 with a BA in Fine Art and Creative Writing (First Class Hons).

She is currently working as an artist for the independent comic book series 'Age of Revolution' in collaboration with Huw Williams, but also works freelance on other art and illustration projects.

Please visit her website for further information and view her online portfolio at

www.h-collins.daportfolio.com

For more information on Age of Revolution please visit

www.cosmicanvil.com

To purchase prints of her comic book art, please visit her print shop on Etsy at HolyGodney.

For commissions and other enquiries please send her an email at h-collins@live.com

You can also follow her on Twitter @SpannerX23.

Chapter One

Dieppe Raid, August 19th 1942

Staff Sergeant Jacky Fisher of the Royal Tank Regiment, attached to the Canadian Calgary Tanks, looked up from the bowels of the Mark One Churchill tank, as his Canadian tank commander Lieutenant Giles Harvey called down to him.

'Jacky, the coxswain wants the motor turned off.'

'She'll maybe not start if we do that, sir; you know she's been a bit temperamental,' Fisher replied.

The workshops had worked on the vehicle until a week before embarkation. The tank was swamped during a training exercise when a large bow wave from a passing landing craft had washed over the tank, combined with an unknown scour in the sandy floor that the Churchill had dived into, cause the water to pour in through the open driver's hatch. The Churchill had subsequently been unceremoniously hauled from the shallows as the tide receded and on to the beach on the Isle of Wight. Although the self-starter was changed and all the electrical wiring dried, the tank's engine often refused to fire without the aid of slave batteries and ether puffed directly into the inlet manifold. These operations had proved in the past to be impossible at sea. Jacky had suggested that the engine was left running while at sea. They carried spare petrol in an outside locker and could top up the fuel tank if necessary.

'He's adamant, Jacky; he says we're smoking him out,' Harvey replied.

Their tank was second in order of disembarkation. Behind them was the armoured Caterpillar bulldozer, "Lula". This machine was tasked to heap up the shingle from the beach against the sea wall, thus to assist theirs and other tanks in climbing onto the promenade and thence be able to penetrate deep into Dieppe's town centre. "Lula", it had been calculated, could also push over the "dragon's teeth"...pyramid-shaped reinforced concrete anti-tank obstacles...at the end of the promenade, that had been seen from aerial photos. Their Mark One was named "Leonora", and its twin-sister in front, "Leopard".

Jacky Fisher was ordered to join the Canadians after a tip-and-run raid by Luftwaffe Focke-Wulf 190 fighter-bombers on Newhaven's assembled landing craft and surrounding waterfront buildings. These ships of "Operation Rutter", as the Dieppe raid was then code-named, sustained only slight damage, but a pub where a dozen Canadian tank-men were billeted was hit, causing many serious injuries, although no deaths, thus creating a shortage of experienced tank drivers. Fisher was a trained instructor-driver-mechanic. He had been familiarised with the Churchill Tank since its introduction to the army, a year or so earlier.

"Rutter" was stood down for other operational reasons

mainly that the high command were convinced the Germans knew of the raider's plans. Fisher returned to his regiment, but a few weeks later, he received orders to retrace his journey to Newhaven. The force reassembled now under the code name "Operation Jubilee". The Dieppe raid was back on!

They trained on the Isle of Wight, with their watertight tanks. The vehicles had extended air inlets and exhausts enabling them to "swim" in up to seven feet of water. It was during this time however "Leonora" was flooded.

They had practised evacuating the tanks in the water and on the beach; the five-man crew drilled unceasingly in the actions that could possibly save their lives and this was invaluable when the water poured in.

Back in the Tank Landing Craft, known as an LCT, Fisher revved the engine and when it was at the height of power reluctantly turned the kill switch to "off". The monster petrol engine fell silent, but this action, an old lorry driver's trick pulled unburned petrol into the cylinders. It was often said to help in restarting. Fisher hoped against hope this would be the case. He took a cigarette from his box and lit it, inhaling the smoke gratefully. Joey Bishop, a non-smoker, chided Fisher.

'Those darned things will be the death of you, Jacky!'

'You have to die from something, I don't think they do much harm,' he answered with a laugh in his voice. Fisher drew on the cigarette again, exhaling through the open hatch. When they landed and the battle began it may be some time before he could smoke again.

He had grown to be as one with these Canadians. They told him of their land of plenty so far away from the cold

English Channel they now crossed. His tank commander, a cultured Lieutenant from the town of Port Hawkesbury on Cape Breton Island, had trained as a music teacher, but like the rest of his Canadian comrades answered the call to arms. He had entertained them in their billet in Newhaven, on a battered upright piano, singing and drinking most nights, as they waited for the embarkation date. The rest of the crew hailed from as far and wide as Canada itself.

The LCT with its flat bottom made the voyage to Dieppe uncomfortable for all the closed-up crews, but in their tank Harvey was able to give them an account of events from his elevated position in the turret. The bad news started whilst they still had only a few miles to travel to the beach.

'I see heavy and intense tracer fire out to sea and to left of the fleet,' he informed them. 'There's something burning, but it's too far off and it's slightly misty so I can't really see what.'

'Well that's the element of surprise gone then,' Joey Bishop the gun layer said ironically.

'The Krauts will doubtless be waiting for us,' Alex Barnes the loader agreed with Bishop. Tracer shells flashed noiselessly overhead as the LCT bounced along in the heavy swell. A radio message crackled over the tank's loudspeaker. A shout from one of the Royal Navy crew also alerted them. They were beginning their run to the beach. Fisher's heart started to beat faster and his mouth became dry. He checked his watch 0445hours.

'Ok, close up, we're beginning the approach,' Harvey called down. 'Fisher, start the...'

In the same instant Fisher felt the LCT and the tank

rock with a sound like a dull bell being struck once, and smelled the distinct odour of cordite. He started to crank the engine. He knew as soon as the whining self-starter engaged the engine, she was not going to fire. He was about to swear, when from behind his cramped driver's compartment there came a strange gasp. The remains of Giles Harvey slid down into the turret. He was missing his head, shoulder and left arm. One of his lungs protruded from the remains of his shattered chest. The body quivered involuntarily once or twice and then lay still.

They felt the LCT swing to the right and Fisher grabbed the side of the tank as he thought for one moment the craft would capsize. Bishop yelled down, 'Start that damn motor, Fisher!'

Leonora's engine still stubbornly refused to fire, but from his restricted view of the outside world through the driver's eye slit, Fisher could see the rear end of "Leopard" and from the blue exhaust smoke, he knew that their tank's engine had started without a problem.

'Bishop,' Fisher called out over his shoulder, 'once "Leopard" moves, get "Lula" to give us a shove, let's see if she can push start us.'

Bishop scrambled up into the turret, unavoidably treading on the remains of Harvey as he did so. After surveying the scene outside, he called down into the hull of the tank.

'That's a no dice situation. Ok men, it's time to go, we'll have to abandon ship, it looks as though the Navy crew are maybe all dead, the LCT's bridge is gone and so is the cabin of "Lula".'

Fisher looked out of his driver's hatch and heard "Leopard's" engine rev up, the exhaust smoke increasing, the acrid petrol fumes entering their vehicle, as that tank started to move, but, although his view was restricted by the tracks of his own Churchill, he could see the ramp had not been lowered by the Royal Navy crew. "Leopard" was pushing futilely against it.

The LCT lurched again and Bishop called down. 'Fisher, we're finished. The LCT is beached broadside and the ramp is still up. So I think it's been damaged. Come on, man, let's all get out.'

Bishop sounded faintly ironic in his slow Canadian drawl. Fisher opened the side hatch on the right-hand side of the tank. He was protected by the hulls of both the LCT and the Churchill. Fisher scrambled out; he saw the water was several feet deep and barrelling fore and aft as the boat rocked in the surf. The ingress of water indicated that the inner door and probably the ramp of this Mark 4 LCT were indeed damaged. Bishop pointed towards the stern of the craft as he joined Fisher.

'Let's get up there and see if we can get this boat's motor started,' he shouted above the battle noise, 'maybe we can reverse off and either try again or get off the beach and then get the hell out of here.' There were constant ricochets of heavy machine gun bullets from the defenders. The crew of "Leopard" joined them.

Its commander was Major Phil Jackson, their section leader. His command flag still fluttered from his now impotent tank's radio mast. He immediately took charge and ordered the men to investigate the situation on the bridge. The swell was rocking the LCT much worse now as they moved cautiously towards the obviously shattered stern. This area was a charnel house. The bloody remnants of the Royal Naval crew washed about in the seawater. One sailor, his "tin hat" still firmly in place, the chinstrap holding it firm, stared at Fisher with accusing dead eyes. Fisher found he was treading on their previous brothers-in-arms; the blood stained the seawater, and that leaked into their boots. The engine room too was flooded. All the essential equipment was below water, an oil and fuel mixture floated in a rainbow-coloured layer on the water's surface. Where the semi-armoured cabin of "Lula" had been, there now protruded some bent control levers and the lower part of the torso and legs of the driver. This man, Fisher and the rest of the tankers had all smoked and chatted together just before boarding the landing craft. It all seemed an age ago.

Bishop reported to Major Jackson, 'LCT's finished sir!'

The officer made the decision. 'There's only one way off and that's over the port side at the stern.' He touched his own flotation jacket, 'use these to stay afloat and try and get yourselves to the beach, we can re-join the main force and at least find out what's happening.'

The LCT lurched in the waves again and at the same time, the German gunners in the static tank turned their attention to them. A shell ricocheted from the turret of "Leopard" and whinnied away unseen into the sea.

They took off their boots at the Major's insistence, knotting the laces and hanging them around their necks. They all had discarded their heavy battle-dresses and re-donned their flotation jackets. This done, they slipped into the heavy swell. It rocked them and threatened to throw the swimmers towards the hull of the LCT, but then in turn threatened to drag them away from the beach and out to sea as the tide was now turning with vicious speed. The LCT was not fast on the beach and swayed dangerously, threatening to turn turtle as the tide receded and the acute slope of the exposed shingle increased.

Fisher was a strong swimmer, having learned on family holidays in the warm waters off Southend-on-Sea and Clacton when he was a child, but the low temperature of the sea and the weight of his remaining uniform immediately took its toll on him. He knew it was every man for himself and he struck out for the shore, his boots quickly floated free from his neck and he was unable to grab them as they slowly sank. Several times, he was aware that bullets had struck the water near him. Fisher saw that one of the young Canadians was immediately swallowed by the cold sea; Fisher noted his own kapok jacket was not as effective as had been claimed, but wondered if the soldier was also struck by enemy fire.

He knew, from their time in training, that many of these young men from across the ocean, fired with a passion to fight for the "mother country", had never even seen the sea, let alone swum in it. Using the last of his strength, Fisher made it to the beach, he had been able to doggy paddle using the sea bottom to guide his way for the last few yards, thus choosing the best spot to land. Two dozen yards up the beach, a stranded tank deflected some of the enemy fire and a number of men sheltered behind it; however, the withering crossfire still raked the shoreline, the shingle between the survivors and safety now a killing ground.

Dozens of bodies rocked in the receding water's edge, others lay where they had fallen further up the beach. He pulled himself into the shallows, his legs heavy from his soaking garments, his mouth, throat and stomach burning from the salt water. The cold was extreme and he knew he should shed his waterlogged battle-dress trousers, but realised he would need them to protect his legs on the beach's gravel. He used the body of a Canadian soldier as a shield while he slipped his sodden kapok flotation jacket off, also to survey the route he needed to take to gain the safety of the sea wall. He pulled the dead soldier's rifle from its death grip; also he removed some pouches of ammunition from the corpse's webbing belt. He ejected the rifle's magazine and examined the bullets. This young Canadian had journeyed halfway across the earth, and, after months of training, had not been even able to fire a single round in anger. He also removed the dead soldier's water bottle and drank greedily from it. He felt the burning pain from the seawater in his stomach recede a little, but immediately retched, spewing the contents of his stomach into the surf, thus relieving some of the soreness. He took another swallow from the canteen and felt the relief from the sweet, cool water.

He saw several other tanks were stranded on the steep shingle; their tracks had been struck either by anti-tank projectiles or had, it seemed, simply fallen from their drive sprockets, having fought in vain for purchase on the gravel. One of them that had made it further than most, before being disabled on a flatter part of the beach and was still able to transverse its turret, thus engaging the concreted-in tank. This vehicle was a pre-war French designed behemoth. Fisher, as a tank man, thought this enemy idea an unusual arrangement. This tank had, like the disabled Churchill, a limited field of fire. Its shells though seemed to bounce off the Allied tank's armour, as did other weapons that the defenders fired from their dugouts and bunkers.

The Churchill's engine compartment was facing towards the sea so, as long as its ammunition and fuel lasted, it would be able to provide response to the defenders. Scattered among these crippled armoured Goliaths were the prone figures of dead Canadian soldiers who had made it further up the beach than most, although many survivors were sheltering behind these wrecks, as the unceasing, withering enemy fire still swept the beach.

He could see the shingle reacting to the ricocheting machine gun shells, as if to enhance their effectiveness, as it caused the pebbles to shatter into thousands of razor sharp flint-shards. Keeping his head low, he allowed his steel helmet to deflect most pebble-shrapnel, as he now thought of it, although one struck his right ear and he felt warm blood begin to course down his neck.

He kept his head tilted forward as he slowly crawled up the beach, his wet stocking feet painfully pushing against the fluid-like shingle. He rested frequently, cautiously raising his head to peer from under his helmet to judge his progress. His leg muscles burned from the exertion, and also from the seawater-soaked trousers. As he progressed further, not believing his luck to escape the attention of the defenders, he was suddenly aware that the beach had become quieter; he could still hear the whinnying of the bullets as they swept the area, but it wasn't near him.

He realised he had reached the shelter of the sea wall and was protected from the enemy gunfire by the angle of its overhanging lip. He scrambled the last few yards oblivious to his wounded feet. A sorry and motley collection of various ranks cowered, almost hugging the protective concrete wall. A medic was attending to a prone figure whose head and left shoulder were encased in blood soaked bandages and field dressings.

Fisher reached into his pocket, took out the watertight cigarette tin and prised it open. He hoped the halfpenny box of matches wrapped, as were his cigarettes, in oilcloth would light. He took them out, placed one in his mouth and struck the match. He cupped his hands around the precious flame as it found the end of the tobacco, sucking greedily on the smoke as it ignited, causing him to cough violently; however, he felt the nicotine immediately release the pent up sugars in his blood.

He undid a second small piece of oil cloth revealing a miniature portrait of himself, his wife Victoria and their baby daughter Harriet. They had spent some precious savings in a photographer's studio in Chelmsford. A larger copy was located in a silver-plated frame on the mantelpiece in their small house in Boundary Road. He also knew his official regimental picture stood in an identical frame to the right of their mantle clock. Folded neatly in the bottom of the tin was the last letter he had received from Victoria before embarkation, this with a smaller piece of faintly lined paper on which Harriet had scrawled with wax crayon. Fisher drew on his cigarette again whilst repacking the items and snapped the lid closed; suddenly he retched more seawater from his stomach.

He looked off the beach towards the horizon. There seemed to be much fewer ships than he would have expected. He could see his own LCT, which was now burning fiercely; it would not be long before the flames found the fuel tanks in the armoured vehicles along with their stored ammunition. The tanks and the bulldozer, if they survived, would be a gift to the Germans, but the amount of slightly damaged vehicles on the beach would leave them in no doubt as to the strengths and weaknesses of Britain's latest battle tank.

Suddenly a Spitfire flashed over their heads, trailing oily-black smoke, its engine running badly with the exhausts popping as it misfired. Two sleek German fighters – Fisher at once recognised them as Focke-Wulf 190s – streaked after the wounded RAF war-bird; their guns and cannon blazing as the Spitfire headed towards the safety of the Allied flotilla's anti-aircraft gun umbrella. The enemy fighters spent shell casings scattered across the shingle. The British aircraft, however, lost its fight to remain airborne, as the damaged engine cut out, causing it suddenly to lose height and splash into the sea, bouncing twice like a skimming pebble, before settling in the water about a mile and a half off shore. He could clearly see the pilot quickly exit his cockpit, first kneeling on the wing, as he inflated his dingy and then scrambling into it, as the weight of fighter's heavy engine caused it to quickly sink beneath him into the sea. Its tail plane however stayed protruding from the water for several minutes like a buoy.

Using this as a beacon a destroyer swung towards the Spitfire's position, its anti-aircraft guns blazing; one of the sleek German fighters wheeled round as if in fright at the ferocity of the weapons on the small warship. Fisher could clearly see a black 5 on the fuselage, in front of the hated black Balkan cross. Too late, with its underbelly exposed to the ship's Pom-Poms it was almost a foregone conclusion. Smoke billowed from its engine momentarily before the fuel tank exploded. The burning petrol surrounded by acrid black smoke hung like a deadly flower as the remains of the plane with its pilot plummeted into the ocean. The Focke-Wulf's compatriot flew off towards the beach; the pilot contented himself with strafing the shoreline before heading off possibly to his base. The destroyer meanwhile had slowed for a few minutes and the RAF flyer pulled aboard.

The Royal Canadian Navy ship was not having all its own way though, as Fisher heard heavy detonations from a shore-based battery on the cliffs above them, and corresponding splashes of shot bracketed the warship. The destroyer, however, was soon was underway again and zigzagging out of range of the enemy guns, its funnel laid a smokescreen, as the captain ordered excess oil to be added to the engine's exhausts.

Fisher's attention was distracted from this battle of life and death played out before them. A medical orderly touched Jacky's arm, bringing him back to reality. He pointed to Fisher's blood-soaked shirt and head.

'Let me bandage that for you, soldier,' he said in a soft Canadian accent, as he looked at Fisher's bloodied feet and remains of his socks. 'Do you know your boot size?' he asked. 'We have lots of spare boots; these boys, well, they will not need them anymore,' he said sadly, looking at the row of dead, their faces covered by blood-stained cloths or their steel helmets.

Fisher sat back smoking while the orderly went about

his work. He told Fisher of their plight and how the Germans were waiting as the first of the landing crafts beached. The medical officer's armoured car was disabled on the shingle, the officer himself becoming a casualty in the first minutes of the landings.

★

About an hour later, the shooting on the beach, having died down as the parties realised their stalemate, finally stopped altogether. The period of silence was broken only by the sounds of fighting in the distance. The Churchill on the beach closed its engine down and the hatchway cautiously opened. They had all heard a heavily accented voice calling from the direction of the German forces.

'Englanders, show yourselves. The fighting is over; your compatriots have left you. Raise your hands and lay down your weapons, and you will not be harmed.'

The figure in the turret of the Churchill tank shouted across to the men sheltering under the seawall.

'They are showing us a white flag.' As he spoke, he climbed down, followed closely behind by a second man, then the side door on the tank opened and three more figures emerged.

A voice from further along the sea wall raised a wry smile among the men gathered near Fisher by saying.

'White flag! Have the Jerries surrendered? And we're not all Englanders, mostly we're Canadians!'

Looking at the bodies, wrecked tanks and landing craft as he stood, Fisher could not feel any humour in the day so far. However, he felt himself laugh along with the irrepressible Canadians.

Fisher could see that the Germans with the white flags were medical orderlies; each wore a white linen jacket with a red cross on each arm, and they appeared to be unarmed. Slowly men began emerging from the shelter of tanks or from the safety within them. As he stood he looked over the sea wall. It had a barbed wire barrier strung on steel supports. He could see that a Churchill, factory-new from the look of it, had made it as far as the "Dragon's Teeth" at the end of the promenade, but was halted there when a track was blown off.

The crew emerged with mugs of tea in their hands. It later transpired that they had been disabled and after they had expended their ammunition they had simply brewed up mugs of tea using the tank's electric kettle, and eaten their rations. The driver – Fisher recognised him – examined the broken track impassively whilst sipping from his enamel mug. He then followed the rest of his crew towards the German troops and captivity.

The German medics divided them into their groups. Seriously wounded, walking wounded, which is where Fisher found himself, plus unwounded, and of which there were only a very few. These remaining Canadians were marched past as a German propaganda news camera recorded the events. The Canadian medics joined with their enemy counter-parts in an unspoken alliance.

Fisher sat on the stone steps of an important-looking building, perhaps the town hall, whilst a news crew filmed the captives for broadcast back in Germany. They would doubtless be sending images of the stranded tanks and landing craft, along with the bodies of the fallen.

Hitler and his high command, Fisher thought, would

be elated at the raid's failure and the capture of so much equipment.

His head was bandaged with a fresh dressing and he was escorted with a number of other captives to a school exercise yard, with a tall chain link fence around it, where the Germans had set up an ad-hoc prison cage. A truck arrived with a Spandau heavy machine gun and crew on its cargo platform. It indicated to the allied troops that their captors would stand for no nonsense.

Later on the Germans bought a mobile field kitchen mounted on an Opel Sturm truck fitted with a canvas tilt. This vehicle was reversed into the school yard. After forming a queue they received a mug of bitter black coffee, and hunks of stale bread. Fisher and his fellow captives were introduced to the fatty canned meat they would soon know as "Old Man", and often rancid Italian soft cheese that they squeezed from cardboard tubes. Fisher found he was ravenously hungry and bolted the food down. He felt nauseous later and regretted his actions after emptying his stomach contents on the asphalt surface of the school's play area. There was a method in the Germans' generosity, as the prisoners found out soon enough.

They were interrogated as to their name, rank and serial number; they were photographed and fingerprinted before being trucked to a nearby railhead next morning, and entrained. The physically and mentally exhausted men who had already spent the night under the stars in the open schoolyard were then forced to endure several days travelling through Occupied Europe, in either freight or cattle trucks before arriving near the German capital, Berlin.

As they were processed before boarding the train, it was obvious to Fisher that the Germans were ill-prepared for the sheer weight of prisoner numbers. Not only were the Germans burdened with the wounded, who were cared for after being dispersed to medical facilities throughout the occupied continent of Europe – the more seriously injured were treated closer to Dieppe – but there was also the problem of housing and feeding over one thousand men in one go; along with over nine hundred allied soldiers that were requiring a grave and a headstone.

Chapter Two

Prison Camp

Eight months later and Fisher was languishing in the same prisoner-of-war camp where he had been taken after disembarkation from the long rail journey. Some of the prisoners had been trucked on to other camps.

A second compound was built adjacent to theirs. A third camp could be seen under construction; the Kreigies, short for Kreigesgefangenen or prisoners of war, could observe the progress as they pounded the "circuit", the compacted earthen path that the Kreigies used as an exercise and a conference area, unheard by the guards who patrolled within the camp. Fisher supposed it was being readied for a new influx of prisoners. They could however call to the closer camp's inmates to hear any news from home or of the war from recent captives. The sky above Berlin was often illuminated by searchlights and the flash of high explosives and the glow of incendiaries, as the RAF began to pound the German capital by night. The group of camps were not far from an outer suburb of Berlin and the prisoners often saw the high-flying bombers of the

USAAF, their contrails indicating their great altitude, although the formidable flak defences blazed away at them. They avoided bombing Berlin and were obviously seeking targets far deeper into Germany.

The Nazi gaolers had coerced many of the prisoners to help clear up bomb damage in their capital's centre and its suburbs. Rewarded as they were with cigarettes and extra food, they were also given some freedom, by way of parole, to visit a local bar. Their guards were never far away, keenly observing the men, although it was clear that none of the captives who enjoyed this period of normality were considered an escape risk. Although Fisher could have murdered for a pint of beer or a decent smoke, he had always desisted from joining the working parties.

One day in the late spring, a black open-top Mercedes staff car arrived outside the Kommandant's office. The camp guards were not front-line troops but were made up mainly of older soldiers, veterans from the Great War or disabled troops of the campaigns in Europe, Greece or North Africa, along with some Hitler Youth. These, often older teenage schoolboys, appeared at weekends when many of the others took their leave.

The guards around the Kommandant's office and surrounding compound sprang to attention. The black leather coat of the occupant flowed like a cape as he strode from the Mercedes convertible; the officer seemed to have misjudged the heat after the fresh air of the journey. He paused and slipped it from his shoulders, passing it to the car's driver who had followed him. A man in a loosely fitting camouflage smock and baggy trousers and carrying a brief case accompanied the officer, but after dropping back when the driver had spoken to him, he then walked behind. The two officers paused, regarding the prisoners briefly, as the latter gathered in the compound intrigued by the new arrivals. The Germans continued on to the camp offices.

The Kreigies returned to their daily existence of trying to stay warm in winter, or as it was now, escape the broiling sun of summer, eking out their provisions from the Red Cross parcels that arrived so infrequently to supplement the poor rations provided by their captors.

Fisher knew his wife and young daughter back at home in Chelmsford, Essex, would still be receiving his pay; meagre though it was, it was more than the conscripts would receive. The Camp Adjutant had told the prisoners they would receive back pay once they were repatriated after the war. He, like Fisher, was a regular soldier, a professional, part of the inter-war recruitment, that, though woefully short of the needs of the United Kingdom, at least ensured many trained regulars to instruct those conscripts as they arrived at their bases when the war began.

In one Red Cross parcel a Dundee cake had been well received. The six-man mess that made up Fisher's part of the hut pooled their parcel's contents. The Red Cross itself added some essentials not readily available in wartime Britain.

Fisher sat impassively eking out a cigarette. There had been no Red Cross parcels for two months. The Kreigies suspected that the camp commandant had held back the luxuries to punish all the camp inmates for those who refused to work, although many of the workers bought in cigarettes and tobacco from the town, these were mainly of Turkish origin. Fisher crushed his cigarette out and shredded the remaining unburned tobacco back into his tin. He could re-use this to roll another smoke later.

The compound gates opened and he became aware of one of the so-called Ferrets security personnel in his grey-green one-piece overalls; with these coveralls it meant that they could quickly search a loft or under the prisoners' huts without messing up their uniforms. Two of these Ferrets stayed in the compound during the day, chatting to the Kreigies, whilst watching their every move. One was now heading his way. The camp guards were also swarming into the compound. Something was clearly afoot. The huts were built on brick pillars to dissuade the inmates from tunnelling. The distance from the camp's barbed wire fence to the nearest hut was also in the inmates' estimate too great a distance to try.

'Raus. Raus.' The Ferrets blew their whistles; they were accompanied by rifle-wielding soldiers running into the compound to back them up. 'Apelle. Apelle. Head-count!' The guards and the Ferrets stamped through the barrack blocks, ensuring the last of the prisoners were outside for the parade or "Apelle".

The prisoners wearily stood up and shuffled towards the parade-ground area. The senior British officer emerged from his barrack block, pulling on his cap. Other bemused Allied officers joined him as they strode out, checking their watches. Most of the prisoners had enrolled in the camp's scheme to learn German, which their captors encouraged, notwithstanding the classroom was outside the wire but still within the Kommandatur compound. It was well heated, a definite plus in the harsh winter months.

Fisher heard the senior British officer call out.

'What the hell are the goons up to now?'

Fisher's only contact with the camp's senior officers had been when he and the other soldiers were dumped here. It seemed from their demeanour that these officers were content just to sit the war out. Most had been "in the bag" since Dunkirk and the fall of France, although some, like their guards, were also veterans of the Greek, Crete or North African campaigns. Many of the Ferrets would spend their time re-hashing the battles and skirmishes they had fought in with these men. All the time they were collecting information, watching, waiting, for the Kreigies to slip up. Apart from a few "gung ho" officers, attempting to escape early on in their incarceration, there had not been too much to bother any of the camp staff.

On these snap Apelle occasions, the prisoners assembled into lines and counted. They now desisted from their "goon baiting" activities, such as moving ranks to increase or decrease the number of prisoners. Once, during the winter months, the guards kept them standing in cold, driving rain, whilst a contingent from the Hitler Youth rummaged through barracks, destroying photos, precious letters and other mementos from home. Vital, hoarded chocolate, tea and tobacco were also stolen.

These younger guards were too young to join front-line service, but nevertheless wished to show their allegiance to the Fatherland. The Kreigies were treated to a display of Nazi cold-heartedness. Fisher started to pull himself to his feet to join the parade.

'Not for you today, Staff Sergeant Fisher,' Oberfeldwebel Max Scheopel said as he paused in front of Fisher before dropping to his haunches, 'for you I must have a special request.' Scheopel, as a veteran tank man, had several times tried to gain Fisher's trust. The German had lost his left arm in one of the many tank skirmishes outside the Libyan town of Tobruk. He often spoke of the strengths and weaknesses of the Churchill tank. When Fisher had asked him the fate of the brand new Churchills at Dieppe, Max had told him after the beach was cleared, many of them were taken back to Germany for evaluation but then used as target practise for a new Panzer, as Max described it. He slipped the word "Tiger" in once, but quickly covered his mistake with a joke saying that the Nazi tank men were Tigers when they fought. Fisher reported the slip to his officer but, he thought, nothing much came of it.

'What can I do for you, Max?' Fisher answered in German. He normally did not stand, or show Scheopel any interest or respect. In the past, Max had tried the "Pally, pally" act towards the incarcerated allied tankers, but everyone suspected Scheopel's intentions. A few had "fed" the German false information in return for extra rations or tobacco. 'What's the fuss about?'

Max listened to Fisher's rendition of the German language. He turned the corners of his mouth down and shrugged his shoulders. 'Still in need of work, Jacky,' he jokingly scolded. Then he laughed: 'No, really, very good. Sehr gut, sehr gut, as we would say. Now what would you say to a cigarette, Jacky?' the German asked.

Fisher looked and could see they were English from the packet, Players, a rare sight after the usual Turkish cigarettes. He reached up and took one. Scheopel did not retract the cigarettes shaking the packet indicated Fisher should take another by moving them closer to Fisher's hand, which he did. Fisher could feel the looks of the assembled Kreigies.

'I have someone who would talk with you; will you accompany me to the office?'

Fisher looked across at the sun-bleached-dry-earth that separated the compound and the administrative offices on the other side of the wire. He took his tobacco tin from his battle-dress pocket and placed the cigarettes in it.

Max upped the stake to encourage Fisher to comply. 'I believe there is tea or coffee, biscuits or maybe some chocolate if you would come,' the German added.

Fisher pushed himself to his feet and dusted his heavy battle-dress trousers down. He said, 'Lead on, Max.' With two cigarettes and the promise of a mug of tea, Fisher knew there was something afoot.

They reached the main gate; Fisher looked around at the ranks of Kreigies still awaiting the head count as he left the compound. An adjacent picket gate set in the wire swung open. The guard, one of the Hitler Youth dressed as they all were in immaculate black uniform, looked incredulously at Fisher, but said nothing; Fisher felt a chill pass through his body as the young trooper's cold eyes cut into his soul. The excursion, it seemed, was all was pre-planned.

He turned and looked at the camp from this vista. High above in the watchtowers and shaded from the early spring heat by the large roofs, the guards, minus uniform jackets, and with their shirtsleeves rolled up, watched with disinterest as the captive soldiers were now being counted by their comrades-in-arms. The fearsome night-patrol dogs panted in their kennels, as hot as their masters in the guardroom were. One of the dogs looked up as it gulped water from a large metal bowl to snarl at Fisher, its ferocious teeth dripping a mixture of water and saliva. The Spandau heavy machine guns hung impotently, as did the searchlights; neither was required on this increasingly baking hot day, on the plain south of Berlin.

★

Scheopel and Fisher entered the office, it exuded an odour of baked wood and tar from the hot roofing felt and also stale cigarettes; Jacky Fisher was immediately aware of a figure at the desk. He had seen the man, who had originally been adorned in the flowing leather coat, who now sat resplendent in the black uniform of an Oberst; a colonel of the Waffen SS. Jacky noted that the officer had an embroidered patch on his left arm. It was a Union Jack. He wondered why or how this was so. Fisher looked at the other person seated at a desk in the corner of the room, which, judging by the heavy typewriter would have normally been occupied by a secretary. The man in the camouflaged uniform also had the death's head of the Waffen SS on his collar.

'Jacky Fisher,' the Oberst stated.

Fisher stared incredulously at the man.

'A problem, Staff Sergeant Fisher?'

'No, for one minute I thought you were—' he paused but then continued '—English?'

The man replied, touching his rank insignia. 'That's for one minute, I thought you were English. Sir!'

Fisher stiffened to attention and was about to repeat the man's instruction, when her saw the Oberst's face break into a grin. He motioned to the chair opposite inviting Fisher to relax. 'You're right of course,' he consulted the folder on the desk in front of him, 'Jacky, I see, Jacky Fisher. Yes, I am British. Originally from Birmingham, but I grew up in Portsmouth. My father, you see, like yours was a sailor too. Your eyes ask questions, Staff Sergeant. My name by the way is Ernest Williams. I was an officer in the Suffolk regiment.'

The door near thc corner of the room opened and the driver Fisher had seen earlier entered with mugs of tea.

'Yes, I wondered how you ended up in the German army. Did you have connections in here? Also the Union flag?' Fisher touched his own left forearm to emphasise his statement.

'Not at all. I was captured in Belgium. A scouting force put us in the "bag" well before the battle for France. I, was in fact one of the original Kreigies. Along with a few RAF personnel, Wellington crews from some raids, in the Hamburg Roads, as I remember. Corporal, or as he is now, Unteroffizer Reynolds here was my driver then, as he is today.' The driver nodded at Fisher. Reynolds also wore a Union Jack patch on his left arm. 'But you're wondering about all this.' He touched the uniform and the black leather holster, from which the butt of an obviously genuine pistol protruded. 'The proposition I shall put to you today will perhaps change your life.'

'We have records telling us that in the mid-thirties

before you joined the army you were a supporter of Oswald Mosley. The German people, you see, Sergeant Fisher, are if nothing, but great record keepers.'

'Yes that's true. But—' Fisher paused to compose himself before continuing '—what has that to do with me here in this prison camp? I didn't like the way Mosley was going; I had some Jewish friends, from school, good friends at that. Their parents were very kind to my mother and myself after she was widowed in the Great War. The "Black Shirts" wanted me turn against them.'

Williams held his hands up to end Fisher's speech. 'But do you still hate Bolshevism and all it stands for? Before you answer, tell me this, you say friends from school. According to our records, that was King Edward V1 Grammar School for boys in Broomfield Road. Shall I quote the motto?' The officer looked over the folder into Fisher's eyes.

'Whatsoever thy hand findeth to do, do it with thy might.' Fisher spoke before Williams could.

'It all must seem a long time ago Sergeant Fisher. You are obviously a man of intellect or you wouldn't have attained such a lofty "alma mater". I was also a grammar school boy, but I went on to Sandhurst and thus became an officer. You had no similar aspirations?'

'I am the son of a Royal Navy officer. My father was killed, as you probably know, during the Great War. The navy sent me there. I wasn't a particularly bright scholar; they gave up on me, I suppose. I joined the Royal Tank Regiment, my intellectual background, given to me by the school, made me appear brighter than the others and got me these, and—' he touched his sergeant's stripes '—they kept me well away from the front line, the fall of France and Belgium and then Dunkirk. Not that I wanted that of course, but as an instructor I was more of an asset in training conscripts. All that of course fell down when the Dieppe Raid came along.' Fisher paused and shrugging his shoulders and then continued, 'In answer to your question it hadn't occurred to me. I've been, like the rest of the prisoners here, more concerned with eating enough and having plenty of tobacco. What Joseph Stalin or his communist hordes do or have done isn't in the forefront of my mind just now.'

'How would you like a belly full of food every day and enough "baccy" to smoke? Maybe a trip to a bar, the chance of real women, we have some delightful buxom Frauleins willing to strip off at the drop of a hat for the Waffen SS, not a few minutes each week with a certain lance bombardier in block 8 who, I understand, entertains some of the officers and other ranks for cigarettes and chocolate.' He held his hand up to stifle Fisher's protest. 'It is well known, Sergeant. Nothing passes us! You could swim in the Baltic, or Mediterranean depending where you were posted. Tennis, football, any sports you wanted, the German army and specifically, the Waffen SS could arrange this for you. The Germans are very keen on sports and fitness.'

Fisher contemplated the officer's statement. 'How would that work?'

'As I told you I have it in my power to change your life. I also have it in my power to drive out of the camp with you, in my car!'

Fisher snorted his reply. 'It's been tried. The men are

in the local cemetery.' They let a man walk out of here quite a few months ago who was dressed as a guard. You may not know this, but they'd had a few new faces on the camp staff and he thought he could bluff his way out. Well it seemed to have worked,' Fisher shrugged and then continued, 'but later we heard shots. The "Old Man" was told that he was shot whilst "resisting capture". So forgive me if I'm sceptical.'

There was a knock at the door and Reynolds walked over and opened it, stiffening to attention when he saw the other SS officer Fisher had seen with Williams earlier.

Williams spoke in fluent German to the officer. The man came in and sat in the chair vacated by Reynolds who had gone into the anteroom and was busying himself with making more refreshments. Fisher could hear German being spoken by Reynolds to another person.

Williams addressed the newcomer. He looked to the Oberst before replying in German to the senior officer's statement. Williams looked at Fisher and spoke in English. 'This is Leutnant Barr, that as you know the rank is the same as a Lieutenant in the British army. Leutnant Barr is a German; he was asking how the interview is progressing. I've told him I think you will leave with us. Although he's learning, the Leutnant doesn't speak so much English as yet. Luckily, my German is very good; it has improved vastly since I was recruited. It was a prison camp much the same as this one. Now I am British and so is Reynolds. He is my driver and Barr, my adjutant. As you can see, I am superior to Leutnant Barr, as he is to Reynolds. You say it's been tried, Fisher; the difference is they didn't have the luxury of two officers from the Waffen SS. Fisher, if you agree to accompany me today; you will be a member of the greatest fighting machine the world has ever seen!'

'The Senior British Officer, will never agree. It won't be long before the protecting power, Switzerland, will be on your tail.' Fisher was unsure of the Oberst's offer but, he was intrigued nonetheless.

Oberst Williams leapt to his feet and crashed his fist against the desk making Fisher jump and the room echo from the noise. 'Those soft clots, hiding behind their neutrality! Adolf Hitler and the German people allow them to exist! Nothing, I repeat nothing comes or goes, to their country without it transverses Axis soil. With one turn of the screw, we could strangle them. Our fighter aircraft escort their planes across our territories even though we know it is possible they are smuggling escaped prisoners of war or even enemy agents. You won't know this of course, but it's true. So please don't think they won't look the other way over one or two British prisoners being spirited away by the SS.'

He lowered his bulky frame to the chair, seemingly suddenly tired by his tirade towards Fisher. An extremely pretty young woman entered the room pushing a tea trolley. She wore a quasi-version of a Wehrmacht uniform. She smiled at Fisher. He felt a tingle run through his body. It was a second round of hot drinks. Fisher smelled the rarest of odours. Real coffee! Williams spotted a small plate of biscuits and offered Fisher a choice. Fisher took one, noting from the impression on the biscuit that they were "Huntley and Palmers".

'As far as the senior officer knows, you are being taken to the local hospital. For medical reasons he will be told.

He will of course protest that you showed no signs of ill health. Whilst in the commandant's office, he will be offered several glasses of Bells, his favourite scotch whisky, which will numb his mind somewhat, along with a choice cigar. Cuban, I'm told. I've been assured that our U-Boats stop over to restock their supplies, whilst on their war patrol in the Caribbean. These are provided by friendly fishermen. Anyway that is the rumour. As for us, we will leave out of sight of the main compound. So what do you say, Jacky Fisher?'

Fisher contemplated for a moment and then replied, 'I'd like to take you up on your offer, thank you, sir.'

'Splendid!' Williams started to speak to Barr, but the German had understood. Barr reached over and offered his hand to Fisher. The German's grip was strong and Fisher began to warm to the idea of leaving the camp. Williams continued, 'I'll leave you here with Reynolds, he will answer any questions you may have. Leutnant Barr and I have another candidate in the north camp to see.' As Williams stood, Reynolds stiffened to attention, nodding to Fisher to do likewise. At the same instant Reynolds saluted Williams as did Barr. Fisher noted that it was more akin to the Canadian salute than the British. He would have expected the Nazi right-arm, raised version. Fisher was cap-less and so didn't feel the need to, but dipped his head in acknowledgment. It seemed to Jacky Fisher there was a lot to learn to be a member of this Waffen SS.

Reynolds introduced himself as Joseph and told Fisher he hailed from Rotherham. He had worked as a chauffeur to a local landowner before the war, having been "in service" since he was fourteen. They chatted like a two old friends. Fisher told Reynolds of his life before the army and about Dieppe. The unteroffizer also told him how he and Williams were recruited and the pitfalls that Fisher and any others may encounter. He also said that recruits to the British Free Corps kept their rank in the British Army. Also they had passes signed by Adolf Hitler and Heinrich Himmler. They received the same rations as regular Waffen SS and were readily accepted into the ranks of this part of the German armed forces. Fisher felt a burden lift from his shoulders. The two men had drained the coffee pot and finished off the biscuits by the time Williams and Barr returned. Reynolds once again stood to attention when the officers entered. They had with them another Kreigie. He introduced himself as Ernie Peters.

Williams finished some paperwork and the camp's commandant, a stiff Prussian officer, with a withered right hand permanently encased in a tight leather glove, signed the two prisoners over to Williams. Barr countersigned the order, placing the original in his black leather briefcase, which he snapped shut. The carbon copy was left on the desk. While this formality was performed Reynolds had left the office and driven the staff car to the rear of the Kommandant's quarters, so shielding the men when they made their way to the car. The Mercedes had two foldaway jump seats that emerged from the floor with a sharp pull of a leather strap. One of these was deployed by Reynolds. He indicated to Peters that he should use it while Fisher sat in the front passenger seat with Reynolds. They sped away, the Mercedes' powerful V8 engine producing a throaty roar, while the dust kicking up from the large car's rear tyres laid an effective screen behind them, clouding over any prying eyes. Fisher looked back at Peters who in turn smiled. Williams had donned the heavy leather coat and seemed oblivious of two former Kreigies. He spoke in German to Barr who nodded as the Oberst raised his voice above the noise of the wind and car's exhaust.

Chapter Three

Training Camp

The barracks had seen many a soldier pass through on his way to the army after basic training. They could have been anywhere in the world and belonged to any army. But only the Waffen SS, Fisher thought, could train men the way he and the other recruits were. Everything was at the double. Kit was polished, cleaned and polished once more. Even their tin mugs for the Ersatz coffee each morning were devoid of any of their original enamel and were polished each and every time they were used. Their individual plates with their grey porridge or fat bacon slices and black bread, which was what their breakfasts amounted to, were also cleaned in the same way. A metal box filled with soft white sand stood alongside the sink providing the abrasion for this action. The need for cleanliness and order knew no bounds.

When each barrack block was required to produce a sentry, the selected man would be washed, scrubbed and shaved. His hair trimmed minutely to the prescribed length. His SS uniform washed and pressed with boots a gleaming. These were worked by two men who toiled all afternoon, melting the polish by the heat from the barrack's stove. The polish was then was applied by the back of the spoon, until several layers were built up. The footwear was then buffed using the softest of cotton pads.

Then he was dressed with precision. His braces were adjusted with a tape measure for accuracy. The soles of his boots polished and the hob-nails buffed with light abrasive sandpaper. His coal scuttle helmet also shone. Then he was carried to the guard house by three men on their shoulders. If the weather was sleet, snow or rain he would be wrapped in a cocooning eiderdown bedspread. Anything less and their barrack block would suffer. The entire building worked to make their man the best. This was the way of the Waffen SS.

For unarmed combat, a Mr Komatsu instructed them. They gathered in a large circle around the diminutive Japanese man. He wore spectacles with impossibly thick lenses. His lopsided bucktooth grin belied the fact that he was amazingly quick on his tiny bare feet. As he showed his pupils his alien moves, punches, kicks, these were all accompanied by strange cries in his own tongue, his feet slapping on the concrete floor. Six other Japanese men, also dressed in the same pyjama-like suits, echoed Mr Komatsu's every move. After each exercise, they turned to their master and bowed.

Fisher was becoming bored. They had been forbidden to smoke, but the need to do so was overtaking him. The six instructors joined the circle of SS men. A door at the end of the building was flung open and an NKVD soldier entered the room. He was coaxed by six Wehrmacht troopers at rifle point. The guns were fitted with razor-sharp bayonets. Fisher knew the uniform of these Russian troops. They were universally hated throughout the Wehrmacht and the SS and, it was rumoured, even within the Russian army. They took no prisoners, had raped and butchered German nurses, Luftwaffe telephonists and other women and children, officers' relatives caught behind the lines in the Russian campaign.

The man, it would be true to say, was six and a half feet tall and probably weighed in excess of twenty stones. Mr Komatsu stood barely five feet in height and had the same build of a jockey Fisher had known back in Essex before the war. All the SS troops in the room tensed. They had grown fond of the Japanese men, Mr Komatsu especially, with his constant grin. He felt the troopers move forward as one to render him, their comrade-in-arms, any assistance. Mr Komatsu sensed this and held his hands up to stop them. The Russian seizing his chance, thinking the Oriental was distracted, made his bid to attack. The Japanese though was not so easily fooled, balancing on his left foot, he swung his short right leg extending it out like a solid steel bar, catching the giant Russian squarely below the ribs in his voluminous belly. The NKVD man's eyes bulged; he expelled a torrent of doubtless fetid breath, followed by a muted scream. As he did so, the pain from the kick and the momentum of his attack, caused him to sink to his knees. Mr Komatsu's fist was a blur as it connected to the large man's throat. A jet of blood expelled from his mouth, which Mr Komatsu deftly dodged. The Russian with a gasping death rattle emanating from his shattered throat was dead before he hit the floor. The

Oriental man turned to his assistants and the gathered British-born SS men and bowed.

Two Wehrmacht troopers stepped forward and pulled the lifeless corpse towards a loading hatch in the wall. A third trooper waited by the wooden door, which he opened, and, catching the deceased Russian's collar, assisted his comrades to eject the NKVD man's corpse. Later on in the afternoon when the SS troopers departed after their instruction class, Fisher and the others saw an Opel "Sturm" light lorry driving away, a pile of bodies on its flat bed.

The SS men, including Fisher, had been "given" a prisoner to practise on. It seemed to him that, when it came to it, the life of a Russian captive was cheap. Fisher's subject was no more than a youth but he squared up to Jacky waving a knife that he had been armed with by the Japanese instructors. All of the Russians were all given such a weapon; however the SS men were all unarmed. Jacky Fisher feigned a move to his opponent's left, causing the Russian to defend himself by moving the knife to that side. Fisher karate-chopped his enemy's wrist and the blade clattered to the floor, he then swung his hips kicking the Russian in the stomach before punching him in the throat. The Soviet gagged as the British SS man's fist hit home. It was not hard enough though; the Russian gasped, dragging air through his damaged windpipe, holding his throat as he fought to breathe. Fisher felt his sleeve touched as Mr Komatsu stepped in and delivered the coup-de-grace by punching the gasping youth's throat. The Russian dropped like a stone to the floor, dead. Mr Komatsu bowed to Fisher, clicking his fingers as he did so. Another prisoner was pushed forward towards Fisher and was dispatched with one blow. Mr Komatsu beamed, making the strange clucking noises of approval, as he and Fisher bowed to each other.

They practised daily with their instructors, with Mr Komatsu watching over them, tutting like a mother hen, as he and the other Japanese moulded them. As their time came to pass out, they had spent the whole night cleaning their equipment, inspecting each other's and looking for faults that did not exist.

The squads were called to the parade ground. Their NCOs looked them over one last time, checking that each man was perfect. Any less and it would reflect on that man when the awards for best squad were announced. They lined up with the expectation of inspection by the gathered senior German officers, Fisher was shocked to see more Russian prisoners herded onto the parade ground. These were all armed with long bayonets. A line of rifle wielding Wehrmacht troopers once again guided the Russians towards the SS men. Fisher and the others realised this was no drill. With cries as numerous as their nationalities, the trainees spread out to meet the interlopers. The Soviet prisoners soon all lay dead. The SS men laughed with relief, congratulating each other as adrenalin coursed through the veins and hearts thumped in unison.

They soon re-joined the inspection rows. Caps were once again placed on heads, sweat wiped from brows and one of the troopers, who was cut badly on his hand, had his wound quickly bandaged, giving up the chance to visit the sick bay to stay for the ceremony they had all worked so hard for.

Among the gathered officers was, of course, Oberst

Williams. After the last Russian corpse was dragged away by the Wehrmacht troops and flung on a waiting Opel truck, an SS General, the red tabs on his uniform bright in the afternoon sunlight, stepped forward. He clapped his gloved hands together whilst beaming in the direction of the Waffen SS men. He spoke in heavily accented English to the British-born SS colonel.

'You are to be congratulated, Herr Oberst. These men, who you have collected from prison camps and have trained for the Fatherland, are now ready to join us. We need them, and others like them, to throw back the Bolsheviks and when, in the fullness of time, the British people realise where the common enemy lies—' He paused, looking fondly at the slim, blond, twenty-year-old Leutnant, who had shared his bed for the past few weeks. Privately the General was known for his many young aides, but he had rarely encountered such a tiger in the bedroom; however, it was time to move on.

He looked away from the youth and continued, 'Then, they will hang that homosexual Jew lover, Winston Churchill from the railings of—' he paused as if to remember the name, but then added '—the railings outside of, is it Buckingham House, or someplace?' He laughed and looked at Williams who smiled his approval: 'And then join us, with their armed forces, headed by our beloved Fuehrer, to defeat the Communist hoards.'

The General looked around at the BFC men. They spontaneously burst into applause. The General held his hand up to quell their enthusiasm, but still the applause continued. He nodded to Williams, who strode from the ranks of the watching officer hierarchy.

'Gentlemen,' Williams called as the clapping subsided briefly. 'Men of the British Free Corps. Men of the—' His voice rose as the applause increased again. They all knew the words that were coming: 'Waffen SS.' The men were stamping their feet and cheering. The throng of senior officers nodded with enthusiasm as they exchanged their views. Williams beamed as his men burst into a rendition of an SS marching song, demonstrating their allegiance to the "Fatherland" by singing in German.

As the song ended the red-tabbed General approached Fisher.

'Name and rank?'

'Joachim Fischer, Oberfeldwebel, Herr General!' Fisher shouted, springing to attention using the hard 'G' to emphasise his knowledge of German.

'You have sworn to defend the Fatherland, Folk and Fuehrer, Staff Sergeant. To accept orders without question.'

'Yes, Herr General!'

The General turned to the other officers present and, speaking in German, said, 'I am going to give this man an order. Whether he acts as I think he will indicates the willingness of all these British and other nationalities here to serve our Fatherland and Fuehrer. No one is to hinder him. That is an order!' The General turned once again to Fisher, and speaking in English. 'Do you see the Leutnant fourth from the right?'

Fisher peered around the General's bulky frame. 'Yes sir!'

The General unclipped his holster and slid the Walther from its confines. He ejected the magazine showing Fisher the bullets. The officer replaced it and pulled the slide back, thus chambering a shell. He slipped the safety catch to "off", showing Fisher. 'Take this gun, walk over to him and shoot the Leutnant through his temple.'

Chapter Four

On Operations

Jacky Fisher surveyed the wind-blown railway platform and shivered in his thin SS uniform; it was standard *Feldgrau* and it had been issued to him some seven months earlier. It did not insulate him from the cold weather of the Balkan coast. He lit and then drew on a Turkish cigarette, feeling the harsh smoke flood his lungs and the nicotine hit beginning to relax him.

Their arrival at the station had been met as usual by the "Feldgendarmerie", their chests adorned by bright metal "gorgets", the breastplates of their authority. He knew that these "Bulls", as they were known in the regular army, were frightened of no one, although they steered clear of any confrontation with either the regular SS or their Waffen equivalent. Fisher, like the rest of the platoon, had their "Soldbuchs" demanded by the "Bulls"; these were combined pay and identity documents. The "gendarmerie" scowled at the first of the British soldiers in their SS uniforms, but passed them through, sneering at them as they filed along the platform.

Along with the rest of his unit, he had attracted numerous stares from the everyday travellers that they rubbed shoulders with on the concourse at Stettin's main railway station. The chief reason for this was their uniform, regular SS but with a Union Jack patch on their left forearms, below on Fisher's the chevron of an Oberfeldwebel. Also the "Three Lions" insignia was on the left-hand collar tab. This, added to the "Deaths head" on the opposite side, was the symbol of the Waffen SS, the elite fighting force made up, in the lower ranks, they had been reassured, by the Germans, mainly of foreigners. Also on the unit's left-hand cuffs there was a sliver stitched "Britisches Freikorps" in old German script on a black ribbon.

Some days earlier, at the same railway station, a detachment of Luftwaffe troops, in their blue-grey uniforms, were escorting an RAF officer, a Wing Commander, Fisher noted his rank from the man's rank insignia. He looked bloodied and bruised, his uniform blouse was singed and his left hand crudely bandaged. He was bare -headed, showing a burn to the left-hand side of his face and neck. This had been smeared with some sort of cream supposedly, Fisher thought, to assist with healing. One of the Luftwaffe troops sneered at the RAF officer and called to Fisher, whilst pointing at the captured airman.

'Hey, hier ist der Luft gangster. Eine terror fleiger.' He laughed and nudged the captive officer with his elbow. Then the Luftwaffe man saw the British union flag patch on Fisher's forearm and the black SS symbols on his collar with the three lions. His face fell, and then he raised his eyes looking into Fisher's. Jacky Fisher returned a fixed cold stare. The British SS trooper cradled his Schmeisser

MP40 machine pistol over the same arm; the weapon was "cocked" although the safety was on. In the magazine the row of thirty-two 9mm bullets lay sleeping. A further five box magazines were stored in a leather pouch on his belt. His dagger, razor honed, lay waiting in its scabbard.

One could never be too careful. He was torn between his feelings for the captured flyer, his compatriot and countryman. He felt unsure how he would have reacted to the British pilot's guards, if they had harmed him there and then. The Wing Commander was bruised and bloodied, as if some sort of unnecessary force may have been used. Fisher was relieved when the guards looked away from his stare and hastily handed their prisoner a cigarette. The airman looked at Fisher with a hateful glare and contemptuously spat on the floor at Fisher's feet. He mouthed the word "Traitor".

As he waited for the train Jacky Fisher mused on the visit to the dentist a few days earlier, with the spotlessly clean treatment room, the quiet efficient atmosphere and the reassuring odour of disinfectant. The relentless war seemed so far away. The company physician had assured him that he had required some routine dental treatment at his final medical examination before leaving the training barracks. The day before, he and the other recruits had their individual blood groups tattooed on the soft skin near their left armpit. The site was still sore as Fisher was put to sleep with gas for the dental procedure.

While "under" from the anaesthetic, his mind had visited some weird and frightening places. Dreams that were so vivid, yet Fisher mentioned them to no one. His unconscious mind took him from his early life when his mother cleaned and washed in their small house in Essex, watching every penny, eking out his father's meagre navy pension. She earned any extra she could from the menial jobs. The hours when he slaved over his homework. His dream took him to the endless days in the camp and the infrequent letters from Queenie; he knew she tried to fill them with news of life and news of his daughter at home. Included were more of Harriet's crayoned pictures of Mummy and Daddy standing outside a rickety house, with an orange sun. Then the first few letters scrawled as she began to write. He now realised that contact from home was gone. How the camp authorities would explain his disappearance, he could only guess.

The dream carried him back to the horror of the beaches of Dieppe, the days of hunger and thirst on the train across Europe, the camp and then the training barracks, the General, the young Leutnant and the Russian prisoners on the parade ground and their subsequent fate. An address in north London kept creeping into his thoughts. A name he did not know constantly repeated in his subconscious thoughts. He saw too the British Prime Minister, who it seemed tried to speak with him in the wild dreams.

He awoke in a recovery room after these anaesthetic-induced nightmares, his clothes soaked with sweat and a bitter taste in his mouth. A nurse immaculate in her white starched uniform brought him a cool glass of water and later a mug of Ersatz coffee with a piece of black bread smeared with margarine-like spread and a tasteless fruit concoction that he supposed was jam. The dental surgeon assured him, although the procedure was successful, the anaesthetic gas had unexpectedly affected him. Fisher explored his mouth with his tongue but found no sign of fillings or extractions. However, when he checked the time he realised he had been anaesthetised for seven hours. Awake he had a recurring thought; of Lords cricket ground in north London, a district known as St John's Wood. He had never as far as he could recall journeyed to the area. Cricket, although played in games lessons at school had never interested him. He played football not only at school but later at regimental level. He had trialled for Ipswich Town but thought of the army as a more secure occupation.

Jacky Fisher's mind returned to the present. A detail of Polish workers from a nearby factory were assembling on the opposite platform, waiting for transport back to their barracks. There was uncertainty even here, in Germany; partisans could attack the weary SS storm-troopers, possibly killing a few, before themselves being dispatched very soon after. Fisher and the other men from the BFC were returning from a few days extra training under the watchful eyes of Mr Komatsu, their diminutive Japanese martial arts instructor.

Fisher now possessed other skills a few years earlier he would never have dreamed of. At an SS training area, they had been taught stealth approach tactics, the like of which even as regulars in the British Army they had not learned. They entered a wired compound with a fence similar to the prison camp. The similarity however ended there. No "goon" towers, although the fence was electrified. Fisher knew this as he had heard the buzz and seen the white porcelain insulators as they had entered the main gate. There were trees, he knew from earlier visits during the day, plus a few derelict buildings but, on this moonless night the inky blackness hid these features. They were given tight-fitting black Panzer Regiment overalls from the clothing store. No rank or unit markings. A black woollen cap with soft leather boots with rubber soles completed each trooper's clothing ensemble.

Among some vital additions was a pressed-tin spring "cricket" that children the world over had played with in the past. Then, a seven-inch razor-sharp double-sided combat knife and finally a choking wire with wooded grip-ends made from black-lacquered dowelling. Mr Komatsu accompanied them inside the killing ground. He held up his metal "cricket", clicking it. His face burst in to the usual infectious grin, his eyes invisible behind the pebble glasses.

Silence was the order of the day as the guards of the training area opened the gates. The trooper's boots with their rubber soles were all but silent as they split to all corners on entry. As they merged into the darkness, they all clicked their crickets.

Fisher drew his knife and crept along, semi crouching. He could smell cigarette smoke and hear the murmur of voices. Clearly the men in the wired compound were unaware they were targets. The talking became identifiable as he neared the men. He clicked his cricket, not wishing to kill a comrade. The voices paused, but a few seconds earlier the glow of a cigarette illuminated a Slavic face.

No cricket sounded in response so Fisher crept silently forward. He straightened to his full height as he sensed the Russian in front of him. The smell of the raw tobacco and the man's sweat invaded his senses. He could see the outline of the target's head framed against the stars. He grasped the chin, covering the mouth, pulling the head back as he did, and the knife sliced across the man's windpipe, severing it along with the main arteries. The target slumped with a mere sigh as his warm life-blood flowed across Fisher's hand. The other man, sensing his friend's demise, called out in Russian. His voice abruptly ceased and there was a sound of the body being lowered to the ground. A cricket clicked and a voice whispered 'Kamerade', with a noticeable Yorkshire accent. It was Peters, the gunner from Rotherham.

Chapter Five

The Proposal

Oberst Williams summoned Peters and Fisher after their training had completed. There was a sailor in the uniform of the "Kreigsmarine", the German navy. They were left in an anti-room and began by exchanging a few words. Evanovitch or Evans, as he had been was of German parentage and had been recruited by the Abwehr, the Nazi secret service. Evanovitch had lived all of his life in Aberfan, Wales.

His father was a coal miner there but originally hailed from the Ruhr. After the First World War, Wales needed coal miners to replace losses suffered in the trenches and Evans' parents took the opportunity and re-located to Wales. As Evans, he enlisted in the Royal Navy and was a crew member of a destroyer that was sunk by a torpedo in the middle of the night. The crew were not at action stations, and the few survivors were picked up from the icy Atlantic by a Free-French corvette *Mimosa*. After recovering, Evans tried to be of assistance to their hosts but found only a few of the mainly Sierra Leoneans spoke English.

Fate struck again as the *Mimosa*, heading after an ASDIC contact at full speed was herself torpedoed by an unseen U-Boat. The *Mimosa* was struck in her bowels by the "tin-fish" and still at full power was driven under in seconds, the torpedo breaking her back, the sea flooding her decks and trapping many seamen at their stations. Evans and some deck crew were thrown into the water. Along with one of the black Free-French sailors, Evans was able to scramble on to a Carley float.

As the *Mimosa* sank, the pre-armed depth charges exploded as they reached their prescribed level. The raft was flung up and, although it saved Evans, he was knocked unconscious by the concussion of the multiple explosions. When he regained his senses Evans found he was alone, surrounded by the flotsam of his former warship and broken bodies of his recent comrades-in-arms. The horizon was empty as far as he could see, the convoy having sailed on. Evans told Fisher and Peters that he spent several hours forlornly shivering and eating some of the rations stored in stowage compartments on the raft.

As night was falling, Evans saw to his disbelief the same U-boat that sank his ship surfacing a hundred yards away and slowly manoeuvring towards the raft. The deck crew had scrambled from the submarine's bowels and were manning the deck gun and the anti-aircraft weapons on the "winter-garden" at the rear of the conning tower. Korvette-Kapitan Johann Moir emerged from conning tower, pulling on his white-topped cap as a line was thrown to Evans. Four watchmen with their powerful Zeiss binoculars scanned the sea at all points of the compass, searching for adversaries.

'He was a real gent, Johann Moir; I owe my life to him.'

'Didn't it bother you sinking your own countrymen?' Fisher asked.

'We didn't see any more targets. He still had torpedoes left and tradition decrees he shouldn't return. You know they fly a Jolly Roger from a broomstick from the periscope standards? Enemies of the Fatherland swept from the oceans and all that. But their fuel was running low. They were supposed to meet a tanker to re-fuel and re-arm, but either they missed the rendezvous-point, or the tanker was otherwise engaged.' Evans shrugged his shoulders: 'I was one of the crew, but even the regular sailors didn't know why. The upshot was we returned to base.'

'So how did you manage to switch sides?'

'Well I completed the rest of the war-patrol with them. My knowledge of the German language stood me well with the rest of the crew. After I got back Johann Moir fixed things and I joined the Kreigsmarine. I've crewed "S" boats in the Baltic since then, we've had a few skirmishes then with the "Ivans", you know, the Russians.'

Peters asked Evans his first name; he shrugged his shoulders and simply answered, 'Taff.'

They were shown into an office richly decorated with oak panelling and smelling of wax polish. Williams bade them sit and they were offered cigarettes and invited to smoke. The Oberst with the Birmingham accent introduced a slim man with wire-rimmed spectacles and thinning blond hair oiled and combed close to his scalp. Fisher looked into his ice-blue eyes and inwardly shivered at the coldness of the man.

'This is Dr Reiken. He is from the Abwehr. That is our secret service.' Williams nodded to Reiken.

'Oberst Williams has assured me that you three men above all others drawn from the ranks of The British Free Corps have shown total loyalty to the German people and our beloved Fuhrer. I am about to give you some good news. You are going to be, er—' he searched for the right word '—sent back to England, though not,' he searched again for the word, then raised his right index finger, 'repatriated. It will appear you have escaped!'

Peters snorted and shook his head and was about to speak.

Williams held his hand up to silence the Yorkshire man, placing an index finger to his lips to emphasise his wish. 'Hear the doctor out!' His face normally so placid turned red as he glared at Peters.

'We have lost track of one of our most important agents in Britain. The reason you will have appeared to have escaped is that this person is very high up in the British Government.' He looked at the three former "Kreigies". 'We know that all ex-prisoners of war, who complete—' he paused again searching it appeared for the right word '—er a "home run", will meet the British Prime Minister. The person you need to contact stands very near to that man.'

After a short period of contemplation, Fisher spoke first. 'Can I ask a question, sir?' He addressed the Abwehr man: 'Surely you have other agents in Britain who can speak to this man?'

Reiken's pale blue eyes narrowed to almost slits once again, making Fisher cold to his bones: 'I didn't say it was, or was not a man.' He paused and then continued, 'You will not know the identity or gender of the agent until I tell you, that will be when you leave for Britain.'

Peters added his thoughts. 'Don't you have concerns we could shop this person as soon as we're back home?'

In a flash Reiken moved forward and in just two steps was a yard in front of Peters. He had drawn a Walther and aimed it at Peters' forehead, with the safety catch off. 'The German people, Oberfeldwebel, in the form of the Abwehr, have long arms and even longer memories!' He checked himself and stepped back a pace, and the gun disappeared back under his jacket, possibly into a shoulder holster. 'In the case of betrayal of our agent, the British authorities would learn, with proof, of *all* your activities with the British Free Corps. All,' he repeated, his cold blue eyes flicking from man to man. 'Do you understand the implications of this?' He paused again and then continued, 'Whatever information you could or could not provide—' he paused letting his words sink in '—would not stop the three of you gasping at the end of a rope. Do we fully understand each other?'

Williams spoke again, 'Any sensible questions?'

Fisher asked, 'How would we appear to escape?'

'Evanovitch is an S-boat crew member – although you may know them as E-boats—a navigator, among other things!'

Taff smiled at this and glanced at his newfound comrades.

'You will go to sea as Waffen SS men, boarding the boat at Travemünde where it has been undergoing an engine overhaul. It will appear you are a crew taking the S-boat back to Stettin. The other Kreigsmarine men on board will in fact be Abwehr officers. They will take you to Sweden, telling the story that the three of you overpowered them. You will have discarded your German uniforms and will be wearing your own British clothes by then. We will of course demand the S-boat and crew are returned. If they do, so much the better, if not we have three Abwehr agents interned in Sweden. I do not think the Swedes are too bright as a nation, so they will hopefully accept your story. Our men will be able to report on their activities.

'Before you leave for Sweden you will be assigned units. Evanovitch, you will return to your duties at your base, Fischer and Pieters, as you are both now known, will be sent to a Flak unit in the port of Stettin where you will be used until the Fatherland has need of you.'

'Any questions before Dr Reiken leaves us?' asked Williams.

'Has the S-boat sufficient range to get us to Sweden?' Evans said.

'The fuel tanks will be full to the brim. Normally the boat would need sufficient diesel oil to get it along the coast. However, as I said, this is an Abwehr operation. The people at the boatyard will comply.'

The four Britons left the Abwehr offices and returned to their base with Reynolds driving the big Mercedes as usual.

Chapter Six

Posted To Stettin

Jacky Fisher winced at the bitter taste of the 'ersatz' coffee. It was made from roasted acorns, and, although he was no coffee lover back in his home town of Chelmsford, Essex, this concoction, he thought, tasted nothing like he had ever experienced before. Fisher's favourite would have been tea but supplies had been inconsistent since they left the prison camp.

Fisher and several of his fellow British Free Corps comrades had been to Stettin main town the night before. They were all paying for it today. His head thumped and he had fought hard to keep his breakfast of rough porridge-like cereal, and he suspected, sour milk, down.

He had once asked back at the SS training barracks of what it consisted of. Grated old man's bones he was informed. This he supposed complemented the canned grey meat, which was known simply as 'old man' and the Italian greasy bland cheese paste that came in a cardboard tube that the German army, to a man, called 'toe-nail cheese'. There was also bacon and sauerkraut. Fisher's mother had been unable to afford meat on a regular basis when Jacky was in his formative years and he had never liked the taste of pork. Many of the crew also avoided the tray of badly cooked meat swimming in fat that was delivered each morning by a Kubelwagon from the main kitchens in Stettin.

The exception was Peters. He had relished in collecting the fat bacon slices and sauerkraut, which none of the others could bear to eat, from around the mess hall. This room was situated deep in the bunker, well below ground and on the same level as the magazine. Peters mopped up the congealed pig-fat with the black bread, the grease running down his chin as he exaggerated the consumption of the meat. One of the Dutch troopers could bear it no more and rushed from the room, his stomach heaving, and his complexion grey with cold sweat.

The previous evening, along with some other nationalities, German, French, Dutch, and some Spanish, they had trawled the bars and clubs of Stettin. Nowhere was closed or out of bounds to any Waffen SS men. Some of them ended up in many of the town's brothels. Fisher's thoughts were of Queenie and his daughter back home in England, and he took no part. His comrades returned to the bar below the brothel, buttoning their trousers with an exaggerated swagger.

It was true that he had visited such a brothel soon after completing his training in the SS barracks. He was intoxicated both with alcohol and with newfound freedom, from not only the prison camp, where he had languished since his capture at Dieppe, but from the restrictions of the SS barracks, the relentless training, cleaning and polishing. The escape from the constant need to perform everything at the double.

He remembered being ushered into a dark, grubby room above one of the many bars. He looked at the woman lying on the dirty sheets and an equally filthy mattress; he could smell the sour unwashed stench from the woman and her surroundings. She smiled, showing that what teeth she possessed were tobacco-discoloured. Her dirty sweat-stained nightdress was pulled above her hips to expose her red swollen and well used sex, with discarded condoms scattered beside her. It was a world away from his wife, his Victoria, his Queenie, with her laundered nightgown and perfumed sheets, her hair platted just the way he liked it.

He turned and left the room, pushing her pimp to the floor, as the man demanded payment; a small dirk appeared from his waistband and was thrust in Fisher's direction. Fisher snatched his SS dagger from its scabbard, thrusting it close to the man's throat, knocking the diminutive blade from his adversary's hand. The pimp's face turned ashen at the sight of Fisher's weapon. Fisher returned back down the stairs to the bar below; he ran the gauntlet of the mainly good-natured jeers and wolf-whistles from his squad mates below.

He soon immersed himself in the beer and schnapps as he had on the previous occasion. The punishment for catching 'anything', as the medical officer had put it, was severe. Fisher and the rest of the Corps members knew they were walking a tightrope between the Germans and their own compatriots. Peters, the former anti-aircraft gunner from Rotherham, had been in the bag since

Dunkirk. Fisher had enough knowledge of these weapons, along with tank and truck maintenance to keep from being posted further on towards the Russian front; this was before the meeting with Dr Reiken. The two men speculated when the call from the Abwehr man would come.

He and Peters had teamed up from their first meeting as Kreigies at the prison camp's offices. Along with other recruits, they were all instructed in the German language at training school, improving on that which they learned in the camp, but Peters' accent often proved too much for their new comrades-in-arms, leaving Fisher to translate. When all the men had enrolled in BFC back at their various camps, they had been promised that the British Free Corps would only engage against the Russians. This quickly proved a lie as the two friends now worked as gun crews feeding the '88s' as they threw up a wall of steel when Stettin port was attacked, either during the day, by the American "Heavy Babies", as the B17 Flying Fortresses and B24 Liberators were nick-named, or by British four-engine bombers by night.

A film crew had arrived to record their enrolment in the German Army. The Free Corps troopers were filmed enjoying a drink, swimming in the Baltic Sea at the resort of Travemünde, sunning themselves on the beach with glasses of beer or Schnapps. They were also filmed strolling around the nearby ancient city of Lübeck, as well as attending an open-air lecture at the famous lighthouse where a photographer and a news cameraman trailed them around as they visited places of interest. A young woman in a quasi-military uniform got them to pose with their faces turned from the cameras as they relaxed in the sun outside a bar. Steins of foaming beer were raised in salute to the filmmakers, the glasses carefully placed to mask their identities.

Whilst on an afternoon out taking in a few bars using a few days' precious leave, the British pair were surprised when Williams and Barr unexpectedly approached. They were chatting to Fisher and Peters. A photographer enquired if he might capture the moment. All four men readily agreed although they pointed out the two senior officers should appear in profile. Fisher's pose for the camera, however, showed him with his cap at a jaunty angle, a wry smile on his face and the Union flag on his left sleeve thrust forward.

Williams separated them from the main group, and as usual with Reynolds driving, took Fisher and Peters on a journey of some miles to the S-boat repair base where they once again encountered Evans. They looked over the giant torpedo boats, which were either on cradles where they had been removed from the water, their hulls being scraped and painted, or in covered workshops with their guns and engines being serviced. A gantry crane effortlessly moved a completed boat back to the water, ready again for the service of the "Fatherland". The whole area was swathed in camouflage netting, around the perimeter quadruple Flakvierlings waited to deal with any enemy incursion.

Williams quietly told the trio how their "escape" would happen. It was not possible, he told them to "steal" an S-boat from Stettin, as the entrance to the Baltic through the Bay of Stettin and the River Oder was too complicated. It necessitated the use of locks to gain access to the sea.

They left the base wondering when the event would occur. Fisher felt full of trepidation about the whole affair and quietly told Peters so.

Chapter Seven

Under Sudden Attack

Fisher was sharply jerked from his thoughts of all that had occurred in the past few years. The wailing sirens and the unique sound of the quadruple Flakvierlings rattling away on the bunker's concrete roof meant only one thing, the 'Jabos' were back. The 'Red Tails', as Jacky Fisher had been informed these fighter-bombers were known, were piloted exclusively by black African-Americans. Flying in P-51 Mustangs along with twin engine P-38 Lightnings, they peeled off after escorting the Fortress and Liberator heavy bombers to their targets, and then flew in groups of up to ten planes looking for targets of opportunity. Fisher's post was in this command and supply bunker, one of many on the outskirts of Stettin, servicing as it did part of the city's ring of anti-aircraft guns, the much-feared '88s'.

These guns defended this important seaport, along with its arms factories and auto-plants. The latter produced light military vehicles, cars and trucks. However, the '88s' were impotent against the low-flying fighters. These planes were each armed with up to six heavy machine guns, but the Flakvierlings, evenly distributed among the '88s' batteries were capable of putting up a withering wall of fire could rip the sleek American fighters to shreds in seconds.

The previous week one of the 'Red Tails' had been forced to crash-land on farmland on the outskirts of Stettin after suffering such heavy damage. The pilot, although injured, had freed himself from the plane's mangled cockpit by the time the SS troopers arrived. Their officer sneered at the American pilot, a captain, as he raised his arms in surrender, after throwing down his fancy chrome-plated pistol.

At their officer's command, two of the soldiers rushed forward to secure their captive, pinning the black pilot's arms behind his back. The SS Leutnant calmly removed his Walther pistol from its holster and shot the American dead through his forehead, some of his brain matter splattering on the two unfortunate troopers. He re-holstered his weapon and mouthed the word 'Untermensch'. Subhuman. This was how the SS saw the black aircrew that regularly arrived from the sky by parachute or by crawling from the wrecks of crash-landed fighter planes. Most fell into the hands of the Wehrmacht, the regular army. They were handed over to the Luftwaffe for incarceration. Few, if any, survived capture by the SS.

Along with the Mustangs were P-38 Lockheed Lightning twin-engine single-seat fighter-bombers, with their deadly accurate heavy machine guns and cannon. At the time of the previous week's attack, several of these aircraft were carrying so called 'gasoline' bombs. A command bunker further north, Fisher learned, had been destroyed by such bombs. The sticky liquid-petroleum had penetrated into the magazine, via an underground railway tunnel. The flames had spread along the track to where shells were being loaded on to a hoist sending a fireball upwards.

The resulting explosion could be heard for over one hundred kilometres. Nothing, Fisher had been told, survived. Where once stood a bunker was now a gigantic crater. Men nearby, but outside of the immediate blast area who were not killed by the shockwave – when the air was sucked from their lungs – were left deaf by the explosion and blinded by the flash.

As this day's attack progressed, the officer commanding their facility ordered the heavy steel doors to the magazine closed. With the inner and outer steel scuttles covering the gun-ports bolted shut and the main steel entrance door sandbagged, there was nothing the personnel could do but ride the attack out. Their mates operating the light Flak guns atop the bunker and surrounding area had sufficient ammunition. With the magazine closed off, there was no more that could be done in any case.

Fisher's Leutnant, a cheerful former school master who was a reservist from the south of Germany near the Italian border, was looking out of the small observation port to the right of the main door. This door had a heavily sandbagged block of concrete positioned five metres in front of it. The aperture the officer looked through afforded a one hundred and eighty degrees vision, whilst only presenting a very small target.

'The bastards are flying down the valley!' the officer exclaimed.

Fisher looked over the smaller man's shoulder. He smelt the sweat and, he supposed, fear from his German comrade-in-arms. He could not see much for the smoke and the incessant drumming of bullets and cannon shells. He then realised the Flak gun on the roof had fallen silent. There were calls from further inside the structure.

'Englanders, Fisher, Peters!' He shouted out names of others who were summoned in heavily accented English. Their Captain's face and blond beard was smeared with blood. 'Come Englanders and men of the SS, come, now is how you earn your pay!' He laughed ironically, 'Come boys, let's ascend into hell!' The Captain's group began to climb the concrete steps that would lead them ultimately to a ladder that permitted access to the top of the bunker. The Leutnant hurried to join them; Fisher noted the reservist always rushed to be at the forefront of any action.

The Captain took a deep breath and, along with the help of another SS trooper, began to push the heavy steel hatch open. Fisher knew they would be required either to man the Flak weapon, if it were serviceable, or help any wounded. The battle was raging around them in the blazing hot sun. Each man knew that this indeed would be, as their officer had prophesied, the hell-on-earth that probably awaited them.

The man-hatch clanged back and they emerged one by one through the narrow aperture into the glaring light, shading their eyes and blinking after the gloom of the bunker. A scene of devastation met them. They scurried to the shelter of the sandbagged wall that surrounded the quadruple Flakvierling. The weapon's barrels faced skyward, and what remained of the crew was shredded meat and uniform fragments. It was obvious the guns were beyond immediate repair. The shell hoist hatch and loading apparatus had been destroyed, the sandbags around the now gaping hole were ripped open, spilling the sand on to the hot concrete.

Fisher saw a hand and lower arm still encased with an officer's uniform clutching a Walther pistol. He leaned forward to retrieve it from the still warm, but stiffening fingers of its former owner. This saved his life. A Lightning whistled overhead, the quietness of its contra-rotating turbo-charged twin engines belied their power; its weapons scythed the lives of all but his. The sandbags were again split asunder offering no protection from the hail of projectiles. He saw Peters' head ripped apart, his body exploding in a dance macabre, as bullets and cannon shells streamed from the fighter-bomber

The last thing that Jacky Fisher, born in Chelmsford Essex, British member of the Waffen SS, one of the most feared fighting forces at that time, heard, was the whistling of a bomb. It dropped short and exploded on the ground immediately below the bunker. He blacked out as the concussion wave hit him. The last thing he saw as he plummeted down the open shell hoist, before he closed his eyes was the bloody fragments of both the Flak crew and his compatriots from the Waffen SS, scattered to the four winds by the shock wave.

Part Two—Present day

Northern France

An Abandoned WW2 Nazi Bunker

Chapter Eight

War Games

The metallic blue Vauxhall Zafira people-carrier slowed to a halt in the car park at the edge of the forest. "Joanna Lumley", was the voice that the car's owner and driver, Dave Benson had installed on his sat-nav. "She" had directed them flawlessly from the channel port of Calais and on their arrival, announced, "You have reached you destination, sweetie."

They unloaded their gear from the rear of the Zafira and started to change their clothes. Voices from along the track caused them to pause, as a group of Roman soldiers appeared, complete with their Eagle standard, resplendent with purple silk streaming from the cross bar. Their "officer" counted the steps, the Latin equivalent, they guessed, of "left, right, left." The "Romans" barely seemed to notice the SS troopers. The Legionnaires marched by, their iron-studded sandals crunching against the compacted earth of the pathway.

Jim Read was the first to pull on his Waffen SS jacket. He had changed into his uniform trousers after spilling lager on his jeans, whilst they were on the ferry. The English Channel was rougher than usual for this time of year. The Eastern sea-board of the United States had been subjected to an unusually fierce hurricane. The United Kingdom also suffered several summer storms as a result, causing unexpected travel difficulties as Britons holidayed.

He took his forage cap from his pocket and slipped it on before sitting on the rear sill of the Vauxhall to pull on his jackboots. Taking a yellow duster from his pocket, he buffed them even though they were immaculate. He had spent an hour on each one at home the evening before, perfecting their finish.

The third member and leader of their group had travelled independently. "Leutnant" Phillip Tasker had set this group up after he joined a similar Waffen SS detachment in his home town of Ipswich.

Tasker had relocated with his job westwards into Essex and advertised for like-minded people to join a similar group. Most of these re-enactors had appeared as extras or "background artists" in many films and also TV programmes. As it was "his" group he took the equivalent rank of Lieutenant, this being Leutnant. He approached Benson and Read from the direction of the bunker.

This edifice of the Nazi occupation of France had been bypassed by the Allied advance in 1944 and therefore was undamaged and had lain derelict for many years, before the local town saw a source of revenue by renting out the bunker to re-enactment groups and filmmakers. Their only stipulation being that the "actor-soldiers" from German army groups did not enter the local town in their uniforms and that the hated Swastika was not shown at all. These conditions were readily met by the many groups, whether they were British, American or German, and this led to the bunker becoming a favourite of quasi-military troops from Britain and the Continent.

Tasker indicated with an over-the-shoulder gesture with his thumb.

'I see the "Romans" are here again; it'll be OK if a passing spaceman sees us all. It would blow his tiny Martian mind!'

Jimmy Read laughed at the thought. 'When are the others arriving?'

Tasker pulled back his cuff and checked. He realised his watch was still set to UK time, removed it from his wrist and began to adjust it. 'When they get here I suppose,' he answered, 'I still say we should have come in convoy in case of any problems. It wasn't our fault. Smithy could've skived off. I'm sure his firm wouldn't have gone out of business without him. I mean it's Saturday, for goodness sake.'

Dave Benson laughed. 'That's not too Teutonic, Herr Leutnant! You should be more forceful. But Smithy is the boss. He thinks his missus can't do without him. We all know our wives are more than capable.'

Benson stood on the car's doorsill, reached over to the roof box and after unclipping the catches, pulled a portable camping gas ring from its interior. 'I'll get a brew on, lads,' he announced.

Jim Read nodded his approval.

But Tasker cautioned them. 'I don't want that—' he indicated the gas ring and cylinder '—in the bunker. You don't need me to tell you about authenticity.' He expected more complaints, but the pair of troopers knew they were here as part of a larger deployment. This had been organised by a syndicate of re-enactment groups, of which their detachment formed just a small part.

Benson clicked his heels and springing to attention shouted, 'Jawohl, Herr Leutnant!'

Tasker returned his salute. 'That's better. Remember chaps, we uphold the code of the Waffen SS.' He straightened his tunic and brushed an imaginary speck of dust from the top of his already immaculate holster. Concealed within was his prized possession, a deactivated Walther pistol, itself dating from the Second World War.

He had bought it on an internet auction site that specialised in artefacts from that period; he also sourced his Luftwaffe watch at the same site, and although not Wehrmacht or SS, he could say, as part of his character, that his brother, a Luftwaffe pilot, had gifted it to him.

When the pistol arrived, he stripped and re-assembled it, while he fantasised about its origins. Was its war-time owner an officer who fought across the frozen Russian Steppes or a paper pushing officer-clerk who never saw action? Had it ever killed anyone? Tasker knew better than to discuss this with his colleagues in the group.

Just than his mobile phone rang out.

Jim Read looked at his "officer" with a look of admonishment as Tasker removed it from his trouser pocket. 'Herr Leutnant! Authenticity!' he tutted, shaking his head.

Tasker answered his Smartphone speaking animatedly. He finished the call and turned to the others. 'Bloody M25's closed at the "bridge". HGV overturned right across all the lanes. The others have turned around the other side of the river and buggered off home. They would have missed their ferry anyway. What a shambles. But, we'll carry on!'

Read and Benson collectively stood to attention ramrod stiff, causing Tasker to smile. Benson then collected up the crockery and washed the cups at a tap located in the picnic area. These along with gas burner and cylinder were all once again stowed in the Zafira's top box. They would not be used again until much later. Any beverages brewed in the bunker would be authentic. So no tea bags or instant coffee!

Around this picnic site were wooden tables and brick-built barbecues where they would, after the "battle", meet their opponents, an "American Ranger" re-enactment group based in Birmingham England, not Alabama. Before this, US soldiers would be attacking them in the bunker.

After Read reiterated the earlier comment that they should have all travelled in convoy, Tasker thought for a moment. He suggested that although they were depleted in number, they could be three Waffen SS men stationed in a bunker trying to delay the Allied advance. Read raised his eyes and shook his head in Benson's direction at Tasker's idea. It all seemed to be somewhat akin to a junior school playground pre-game plans.

The barbecue would take place at Sunday lunchtime, before that the Waffen SS men would occupy the bunker all night and the "American" and "British Tommies" would attack. After the barbecue, when many photos would be taken with men in their authentic uniforms, leaning on weapons, jeeps and trucks of the period, they would all set off home. A few beers, along with some vital networking with the others from different Waffen SS re-enactment groups, as well as the "US Rangers" and the inevitable "Tommies" was vital, as they would not meet again for some months. Any news of film work would be exchanged. They had all appeared in Hollywood films and rubbed shoulders with big names, travelled to various European cities, seen dozens of one-sixth scale tanks in battles that were all later enhanced by CGI for the big screen. When the film was released they of course attended the local cinema with wives and families. They purchased copies of DVDs on their release. Images were uploaded to their website and links to U-Tube publicising their group.

The crack from the deactivated M1 carbines was nothing compared to the sharp report they would have originally made. It was as close as the Rangers could get in this simulated battle. The SS group replied with rifle and machine-pistol fire from the slits built into the bunker. Even though the battle was false, and the would-be protagonists were soon to be sharing a coffee or cold French lager, as burgers and sausages sizzled on barbecues, they laid into the fight with gusto. The atmosphere in the previously musty bunker was tinged with sweat and gun-smoke as adrenalin from the excitement coursed through their veins.

It was damp and almost completely dark as Fisher regained consciousness. The odour from the explosion was still fresh in his lungs, causing him to vomit. His stomach expelled most of his last meal.

The regurgitated "old man", ersatz coffee and black bread tasted sour as it had mixed with stomach acid, the combination stinging his mouth. It felt from the hot sticky mess – that he tried to catch in his hands so as to prevent it from staining his uniform – that it had barely changed in composition since he had eaten it in the mess room, an hour or so earlier, before the attack on the bunker in Stettin began.

His senses were numbed; along with the red hue before his eyes there was a banging in his brain from the concussive blast and the bright flash of the bomb. This made his head swim as he tried to stand. His eyes fought vainly to adjust to the gloom; the damp sense in his nose was the same odour as the freshly dug soil at his grandfather's grave, still haunting his brain.

As an eight-year-old he had been encouraged to toss his handful of earth; subconsciously he aimed it at the bright brass coffin plate that his mother had so diligently polished earlier that very morning before the undertakers called to collect her father's coffin.

He felt for his heavy "coal-scuttle" helmet that had slipped from his head. His fingers found it lying upside-down about a foot away. He snatched it up and put on his head, tucking the rough leather strap under his chin.

He scrabbled around in the dirt and found his MP40 machine pistol. It gave him the comfort he knew that came from being a member of the British Free Corps, part of the Waffen SS, possibly the most feared fighting machine in any army anywhere in the world. He was ready to fight to defend Fuhrer, Fatherland and Folk.

He shook his head to clear the effects of the bomb blast from his senses. He looked at the familiar, yet unfamiliar surroundings. Jacky Fisher could not wait any longer to examine the area to unlock this puzzle; he ascended the remaining steps to the next level, his iron-studded boots rasping on the concrete. Although his legs and body were tired and ached from the effects of the explosion and fall down the shell hoist, he summoned extra energy buried within his muscles by the intense and unyielding training of the Waffen SS.

This pushed him forward. He entered the main passageway that ran the length of the ground-level chambers. He was surprised to see the store rooms and sleeping quarters; they were usually full of the day-to-day requirements and neatly stowed possessions of the soldiers, but the dormitories, usually with their black iron bunk beds and grey personal lockers, were bare of any furniture. The ammunition magazine's door was unusually open and the entrance to the tunnel where the small electric train normally delivered the ordinance was stuffed with roots. The sound of gunfire, although unnaturally muted, was now more prevalent. As he entered the main chamber he saw three fellow Waffen SS troopers operating at the observation slits, their weapons raised and firing. Choosing an unmanned aperture, he cocked his MP40 and slipped the safety off and looked out.

To Fisher's surprise, he could see American soldiers. Also trees! The apparent invasion of these olive-green clad troops couldn't be readily explained. Fisher's mind was in turmoil, because of the many occasions he had left the bunker to fetch water, supplies or even when they had the opportunity for leave, which meant the British and other foreign troops made their way to the bars and brothels of Stettin, but there had never been Americans.

It was as if he was in another place. The normally bare dusty barren landscape was now thickly wooded, along with grass and other plants in abundance. He could see through the trees brightly coloured cars and vans, also people standing watching.

However, he could not dally. They were under attack and he had to join in the defence. Keeping low, he loosed off a burst of shells. Trees splintered and he was gratified to see the Yanks throwing themselves to the ground; they scrambled away looking for cover. Amazingly, most had abandoned their weapons! The people at the edge of the wood also threw themselves to the ground.

He heard angry shouts from either side; it seemed by the accents these men in the bunker were fellow British Free Corps, although the Union Flag that adorned his own sleeve just above the cuff was not present. Some of the uniform trousers also seemed to be the wrong colour.

An SS Leutnant, his face smeared with green and black camo-face-paint screamed at him.

'Who the hell are you and what are you flaming well up to?'

Fisher immediately sprung to attention, his middle fingers on the side seams of his trousers, his MP40 swung from his neck by its rough leather strap, the magazine prodding against his belt as it did so.

'Jawohl, Herr Leutnant!' he exclaimed.

Tasker stood open-mouthed as the gun smoke from Fisher's Schmeisser gradually cleared. Ejected spent shell casings littered the floor. The interloper still stood to attention. He was looking into the far distance behind Phillip Tasker's right shoulder. Tasker for his part regarded

Fisher. The uniform was truly authentic, the MP40 possibly the best he had seen, a Walther that was tucked into the intruder's belt a twin to his own, but the fact that the machine-pistol had discharged live rounds was a problem. A huge problem. He heard shouts coming from outside and hammering on the steel door of the bunker.

Speaking in German, Fisher suddenly barked out his Army serial number followed by 'Joachim Fischer, Oberfeldwebel, Waffen SS. Herr Leutnant!' He raised his right hand, plucking a booklet from his left breast pocket and presented it to Tasker, who took it. It was Fisher's "Soldbuch". Tasker examined it.

'This is very authentic,' Tasker said appreciatively. Jim Read looked over Tasker's shoulder.

'Where did this come from, chap? They are really bloody expensive, even a fake one. But an example as good as this, absolutely priceless,' Read stated.

Fisher saw that Read was a private soldier and tapped the Feldwebel's chevrons on his arm and raised his eyebrows questioningly. Read appeared to ignore Fisher and said nothing as Fisher replied. 'I was issued it. I'm British too. British Free Corps.'

'British what?' exclaimed Read. 'Those bunch of traitors. Do you remember, Phil, a few years back in the paper?'

'Yes I remember. But, what did you say your name was?'

Fisher was still standing to attention. 'Fischer, Joachim Fischer, Herr Leutnant!'

'You can call me Phil, er...Joachim.'

'I'd prefer to call you Leutnant, Herr Leutnant.'

'Loosen up a bit, chap, this is not the SS, we are only play acting, nothing serious.' Read said.

'Only playing. Acting! What do you mean? Are you not members of the Waffen SS?'

'Not at all, Joachim and can I ask, where the hell did you appear from? As far as I was aware this place is pretty bullet-proof, in more ways than one.' Tasker laughed at his own joke. 'Erm…let's go outside and have a coffee or a beer or something and get this gun smoke out of our lungs.'

Fisher once again suddenly felt faint and sank to his knees; he could not equate with the words these troopers had spoken. He used the butt of the MP40 to steady his descent to the dusty, concrete floor. Once again, his stomach ejected his last meal, the final remains of the "Old Man" from earlier, then uncontrollable bitter yellow bile followed; it puddled in the dust, resembling pale egg yolk.

Tasker placed a hand on Fisher's shoulder. 'Take it steady, mate, I'll get you some water.' He took his canteen from his belt but then thought better of it. The canteen, although authentic and dating from the early 1940s, contained water, Tasker remembered, that had been in it for over a year.

Benson stepped forward, offering a plastic bottle, removing the cap as he did so. Fisher took it and was surprised at its lightness, grasping the container and not realising it was plastic, squeezing too hard. Some of the water was ejected over his hand. However, he raised it to his lips and drank the remaining fluid greedily, feeling the cool liquid wash away the bitter taste of bile. Fisher proffered it to Benson who refused at the thought of the stranger's sputum, some of which still clung to his chin. He told him to keep it.

'So you aren't Waffen SS. What do the real SS think

about this? I can tell you they are not to be trifled with,' Fisher stated.

'The SS? They haven't been around since the end of World War Two! We just enjoy dressing up as SS soldiers. Doing the things they did. We've been in films and TV.'

Fisher looked incredulously at the re-enactors. He snorted his reply. 'Do the things the SS did? You obviously are unaware of the things that we did, my friends. You say World War Two. This morning I was in Stettin and the war was very much on, I can assure you!'

Two of the American soldiers Fisher had seen in the woods entered the room.

'What the hell was that all about? One of my guys has quite a bad splinter wound. You're lucky no one was killed.' The speaker's accent identified him to Jacky as a native of the West Midlands.

Tasker spoke in reply. 'Our friend here literally appeared from thin air, we're still trying to understand how and where he came from.' After more discussions about the wounded man, the "Americans" retraced their steps with the Waffen SS troopers right behind. Read helped Jacky to his feet but found when he asked to examine Fisher's MP40, his request was refused.

Fisher tucked the machine pistol behind him after checking the safety was "on". The group walked from the bunker and when they were a dozen yards away from the concrete edifice, Fisher turned to observe his surroundings. He saw the near-identical structure he had entered earlier that day, before the attack in Stettin.

Tasker led him over to the barbecue tables and indicated

where he should sit, which Fisher did. He removed his belt with its "Gott Mit Uns" on the buckle and the leather pouch containing five more box magazines for the MP40. Fisher pushed it to an unoccupied portion of the table well away from Read, who was still looking enviously at the equipment. Tasker uncapped a stumpy bottle of French bier-blonde lager, and passed it to Fisher.

'So Joachim, tell me about yourself.'

Fisher took a long swig from the bottle, nearly emptying it, he looked at it and nodded appreciatively, and after coughing to clear his throat, began to speak.

'Well my real name is Jacky Fisher, I'm from Colchester in Essex and I was captured at Dieppe. I have to say that along with many other prisoners of war, I joined the British Free Corps. We weren't as you said—' he looked pointedly at Read '—traitors. The members of the Free Corps were offered a way out of prison. Remember we were imprisoned for being soldiers. The food was lousy, nothing much to smoke, no beer. Also we thought there was a way of maybe getting home. Of escaping.'

'This is all too much Jacky. I mean Doctor Who or maybe Arnie in *The Terminator*, or even H G Wells and his time machine. But time travel? It doesn't exist, does it?' Tasker semi-sneered the question at Fisher. 'What you're saying is that you have travelled in time today, to us, here in France? I really don't think so.'

Fisher went to one of his pockets and pulled out his tobacco tin; he took from it a pre-rolled cigarette and placed it in his mouth. He patted his trousers but failed to find his cigarette lighter.

'Does anyone have a match?' he asked.

'Crikey, we can't afford to smoke in our time! If, as you say, you're from the past, which, I for one moment don't believe.' Read laughingly chided Fisher: 'You'll need to know that. Nearly eight and a half quid a packet, mate! And then there's the health risk, but, if you're really who you say you are, you won't know about that either, will you?'

Dave Benson had listened intently to the conversation and without speaking stood up and walked to the Zafira. He opened the door, reached in and took a cigarette lighter from the indentation on the dash. He returned and cupped the flame for Fisher, who nodded his thanks, while sucking greedily at the cigarette, coughing as he did so. Benson sat down again, Read theatrically sniffed at the smoke and exclaimed,

'Blimey boy, what're you smoking there? Smells like old army boots!'

Fisher answered him. 'It's Turkish tobacco, it's all we can get.' He suddenly exclaimed, after exhaling another lungful of pungent smoke, 'Wait! I have a wife and daughter, they'll know me. My wife is called Victoria, although within our family she's known as Queenie. My little girl is Hattie.' He reopened his tobacco box and took the well-worn photos out, shaking a few stray flakes of his precious tobacco back into the container.

Benson took them and placed the family group portrait and the army's photo side by side. The other two re-enactors looked them over.

'What year were you supposedly born then, Jackie?' asked Benson looking up from the pictures.

'Supposedly! What do you mean by that?'

'Humour us, Jacky.'

'I was born on 25th of January 1911.'

'So that makes you,' Tasker completed his mental calculation, 'well over one hundred years old. Your wife Queenie, when was she born?'

'1st of August 1917 and Hattie, she was born in 1939 the day before the war was declared, 2nd of September. I'm thirty-two years old, if it's still,' Fisher paused as if to remember, 'August, as it was this morning in Stettin.'

'It's still August. You mentioned Stettin earlier, but I have to ask where the hell is Stettin? I've personally never heard of it?' Benson asked.

Tasker stood and walked to his car and after unlocking the glove-box, returned with his Nokia smart phone and pressed the touch screen several times.

'Here we are , Stettin, once a German port city on the Baltic, now known as, blimey, I'll have to spell it, lads, Szczecin. Well it's Polish now, so that explains the impossible name. So Jacky, you say that up to today, in fact this morning, you were in a bunker the same as this one, but in Stettin, in Poland?

'Germany, Stettin most definitely in Germany. It was an anti-aircraft supply tower and support bunker, identical to this one in fact.' He swept his arm to emphasise his words.

'So you say you were fighting against us, if all this old bollocks is to be believed, which again, for one minute I don't. So how did you get in to *this* bunker? One thing for sure it's not designed to be accessed easily,' Read said.

'I fell down the shell hoist from the top.' Fisher pointed to the top of the concrete structure.

'Show us then.' Benson stood and walked purposely towards the main door. 'C'mon, clever clogs.'

Fisher picked up his weapons from the table. The other two raised themselves from the benches and followed, entering through the main steel door. Jacky Fisher led the way, pausing to name the concrete rooms as they passed. Eventually he came to the bottom of the shell hoist and pointed up the shaft.

'This is it.'

Tasker produced a wind-up torch and shone it into the dark void. Satisfied he passed it to the two men who took turns in examining the structure.

'Bugger all up there, just steel rungs set into the concrete, if you'd have fallen down that, you would've smashed every bone in your body. What's up there anyway?' Read exclaimed. 'So where's this shell hoist then, Jacky?'

Fisher acknowledged that there was no internal fitting for the hoist.

Tasker spoke, 'Hang on for a minute. This is a type 623 bunker, I'm sad to say I've studied Nazi bunkers since we first came here. It was a basic design that could be adapted. It looks as if there's no shell hoist but—' he shone his torch once again into the gloom '—you'll see the bricked-up portal there, that leads to the redoubt on the far side. The Frenchies blocked it off to secure the main part of the bunker. Through there—' he highlighted the brickwork once more '—is where the main gun emplacement would have been; all this part, as Jacky says, is where the troops would have lived. When D-day came, as we know from the local history, the bunker was by-passed, because the gun intended for it had never been installed. I see from photos of other 623s there's a provision for access to the top for either escape or maybe as a defence position? There's one in Holland on a beach the same as this, but it's been eroded by the sea and fallen over.'

The men returned outside into the sunshine and sat at the picnic benches. Read opened two more beer bottles and passed another one to Fisher: 'How're we going to get Jacky here home. I take it you didn't have a passport for Dieppe, Jacky?' He laughed as Benson and Read opened bottles themselves. They all walked towards the barbecues which had been lit when their mock battle had been brought to such a sudden end. Fisher whose stomach was still queasy from earlier declined the offer of sausages and burgers. He took a soft bread roll and ate it slowly, hoping to absorb some of the bile in his stomach.

'We travelled with our identity cards and of course our "dog-tags".' Fisher pulled his German army tags from the confines of his shirt and rattled them. 'Dieppe was only a raid; we were hoping to return to Britain you know.'

'I read a bit about it at school, of course. I gather it was a cock-up,' stated Benson.

Fisher nodded his agreement.

'Still no matter, Jacky.' Tasker took up the conversation. 'We need to get you back to the UK.'

'So we're going with the premise Jacky here really has come through time,' Benson said, shaking his head in apparent disbelief.

'How do you think we'll get him through immigration? Those boys aren't silly, what with all the illegals trying to smuggle themselves in.'

'I think I should see the army. They will surely know about me?' Fisher suggested.

'Not after all this time, Jacky, well I shouldn't think so, and not done up in that garb!' Read shook his head.

Tasker walked to his car, returning with a passport in his hand.

'The Memsahib, the missus that is left hers in the glove box when we did a booze cruise a few weeks ago; all we have to do is sit Jacky in the back of the people carrier behind the privacy windows, you two wear your uniforms and sit in the front, you'll all look like peas in a pod, wave your passports at the officers. Should be all OK.'

'Famous last words,' said Benson.

Chapter Nine

Under arrest; Dover Police Station

'I'm looking for an excuse or at the very least a reasonable explanation for all this.'

Jacky Fisher looked at the detective as he waved his hands over the confiscated weapons. The guns were now encased in individual heavy grade plastic bags, with yellow printed labels stating "EVIDENCE" on them. His belt and dagger, along with the spare box magazines for the MP40, was there too. Gerome Cody, as he had introduced himself, was first of the black men to address him. He was very black. His head, it seemed to Fisher, was totally devoid of hair and shone like one of the Crown Bowls his Uncle Eric kept under the stairs at his mother's house in Essex.

It had indeed been famous last words as Dave Benson had prophesied. The Vauxhall and its passengers were pulled into a customs shed for a random check. Straightaway their ruse was discovered. Tasker was behind them in his car and also held his hands up to the officials. Fisher's MP40, dagger and Walther were found and seized. The group were bought to Dover police station.

Fisher shrugged, but continued to assess these strange men. The only time previously he had ever seen a black person, was on a film in the cinema when he and Queenie watched *Gone with the Wind*. Those black people were always portrayed as servants or slaves. Then there were jazz musicians such as Louis Armstrong, who they saw on *Pathe News*, with his latest hit songs from the USA.

Both had said they were policemen. They were nothing like police Fisher had ever seen before. They were dressed, it seemed to him, in dungarees, with the knees worn right through, clothes more suitable for road-repair navvies. They wore coloured undershirts with some inane printing on them and a curious design of plimsolls on their feet.

The second black man, well, Fisher thought, brown man, put something in to a box and selected a button. The device screeched, making Fisher jump. The policeman looked at Fisher; his brown face, shining with sweat, had a sour look. He hissed through his teeth as he did so.

The very black man said, 'Interview with Jacky Fisher, present are DCs Gerome Cody and…'

'Michael Stanford.' Brown boy spoke.

'Mr Fisher,' said Cody, 'I'll remind you once again you do not have to say anything, but it may harm your defence, if you fail to mention something you later rely on in court. Do you understand?'

Fisher felt unsure about the statement but before could he answer Brown boy interjected. 'You are very jumpy mate, what's your problem?'

Fisher shook his head. 'I don't think I have a problem. I'm not used to "Darkies" that's all.'

'You say what! Darkies! What the f…' He checked

himself: 'The hell you say. When do you ever call blacks like us, Darkies?'

'I'm sorry, it's just what we call Negroes.'

'Negroes!' He slammed his fist on to the table making it shake. 'Listen, I'm British, born in Britain, mate, we both are. We're both Londoners!'

Cody tapped Stanford on the shoulder, lightly pushing him away. Stanford hissed through his teeth and walked towards the window that overlooked the exercise yard. He pulled the waistband of his denim trousers up but they immediately sagged again exposing the elasticated band of his multi-coloured boxer shorts. He hissed again whilst shaking his head, as he placed his large black hands on the window sill and stared in to the distance.

Cody leaned on the table edge and looked Fisher hard in to his eyes.

'Listen man, you have a very big problem.' He snatched up two of the evidence bags, one containing his Schmeisser and the other the Walther. He held them aloft and shook them in Fisher's direction, before lowering the bag that the pistol was in to an inch away from Fisher's face. He spoke quietly and succinctly to Fisher, 'This is some heavy, heavy stuff man! This is going away for a long, long, time. That's the mire you are in, man!'

Fisher looked confused at his use of words. He started to speak but was cut off.

'Where did you get them? And, listen to wise words, mate, don't say you were issued with them. All this crap about being someone from the past is all bullshit. You reckon you are a British soldier, in the German Army, from World War frigging Two. It's all bull. Bull! You think we are fools? Give it up. Give up with the bullshit, man,' the Black Boy shouted.

Fisher thought of his cigarettes. He craved a smoke, but his requests to light up since he was arrested had been constantly refused. When the Waffen SS re-enactment group had smuggled him on the ferry, and then back to Dover, they had told him that he would be OK once they were back in England. 'Just tell them the truth, Jacky, you'll be all right,' Tasker had said.

Fisher knew they weren't OK though either. It seemed Tasker had severely underestimated the customs and immigration officials. He thought it would be fine to smuggle this man back to thc UK, who had appeared out of thin air, in a former Nazi bunker, in a forest in northern France. He knew his new-found friends were in custody. They had tried to help him and ended up in big trouble. Fisher felt troubled by his thoughts and felt his despair rising.

The men, the brown boy told him, had been convinced by Fisher that he had just appeared. 'I don't know what sort of stuff they are on, but man, I sure hope they've got some left.'

Black Boy erupted in a long bellowing laugh and the two men made fists of their hands. Fisher thought that they were about to fight, but they merely touched their knuckles together. Black Boy looked down and started to speak again to Fisher, but he was interrupted by a knock on the door.

Brown Boy said, 'Enter.'

A uniformed policeman appeared followed by a young woman.

"PC?' Brown boy creased his forehead as he asked the question.

'Wills.'

'Has entered the room,' Black Boy said. He seemed anxious to continue.

The woman spoke saying, 'I'm Pat Banning. I'm your solicitor, Mr Fisher. Don't say another word!' She looked at the two black men and then at the door and motioned with her head that they should leave.

Along with the uniformed officer, the two black DCs turned and made their way to leave the room. Black Boy picked up the bags containing the weapons, and Brown Boy switched off the box, which screeched again. Stanford hissed through his teeth while looking pointedly at Fisher. He gestured to Fisher with his free hand. 'It's not over, so don't think it is!'

Jacky Fisher was not so shocked at the noise this time. He felt comforted with the appearance of Pat Banning, a seemingly friendly face where previously there only had adversaries.

After Black and Brown Boy had left, Pat asked Fisher if he wanted anything.

'I'd kill for a smoke please.'

'Well you seem to have enough guns to do that! I'll ask the custody sergeant to allow you into the exercise yard. I'm afraid you can't smoke in here though, or anywhere in the building. It's against the law. You must know that. It has been several years since it came in. I've never smoked so, I'm glad to say I don't really know how you feel.'

'It's murder, miss.'

'Call me Pat.' She saw the confusion in his eyes: 'My real name's Patricia, but I hate it.'

'Now, Jacky, is that short for John?'

'No. I'm named after a famous man, Admiral Lord Jacky Fisher.'

The solicitor smiled. 'He must be very famous indeed, but I've never heard of him,' she replied with a laugh in her voice.

Fisher explained all the events to her.

'Everything you tell me seems so fantastic. The police haven't had time to check up as it's Sunday and as you'll probably know, or maybe don't, even the Army closes on Sunday. They will want to keep you in custody overnight. I'll make the arrangements so you will be well looked after. I suggest, until we can contact the Army Records Office, we offer what we call a "no comment" to the police.' She explained what she meant.

He was relieved, as he was very tired after such a tumultuous day.

Fisher was taken to the custody sergeant. The charges of being in possession of two firearms, ammunition, his SS dagger and entering the country illegally were put to him. His uniform had been taken away and he had initially been given a disposable white paper suit and paper underwear. He was allowed to use the exercise yard to smoke. He paced around the cold and desolate concrete walled area; a chill wind blew a dust eddy into a small whirlwind in the corner of the yard. As he drew gratefully on the cigarette, inhaling the smoke, he felt the release of tension, and he thought of the freedom both he and the dust eddy looked for. After his cigarette break he was taken to a cell. Later a plate of fish and chips with bread and butter and with a large plastic mug of tea was brought to him. He gave up with the flimsy plastic cutlery and ate the food with his fingers. After the meal he took a final trip to the yard for a smoke, then settled down in his bed.

He remembered being in custody when he was eighteen, just before he joined the Army. A high street shop window had been broken in a boisterous incident. Fisher, innocent and uninvolved, had been scooped up along with the genuine perpetrators, although no charges were brought against him. That short experience of those cold dark rooms reeking of urine, vomit and the heavy smell of disinfectant, with the ever-present damp floors, were a world away from this heated, well-lit cell, with its thin but nevertheless comfortable mattress and warm blanket in which he found himself incarcerated. The paper pillow was comfortable and he fell into a deep sleep.

Before dozing off, Jacky Fisher reflected on his first day in this modern world. It had started decades before with him and his mates fighting for their lives in Stettin, on the Nazi-German Baltic Sea coast, and then incredibly had him joining new friends in France, finishing in a cell located in, as he had been told, Dover police station.

Chapter Ten

Back to the Army

The next morning Pat Banning returned with some clothes. She gave him three grey T-shirts, a black hooded fleece top and matching jogging bottoms, a six-pack of socks and a pair of cheap trainers with Velcro fasteners. He asked how he would pay for them but she said it was his right as his uniform had been confiscated. When they returned to the custody area, there was no sign of the two detectives. Fisher asked about them, but his solicitor told him they were Counter Terrorism from London.

Enquiries had been made with the Army and as such they had no more interest in him. He was bailed into the custody of the Army and released. Pat Banning completed the forms and showed Fisher where to sign. She was given copies of the cassette tapes in a clear plastic bag.

They left the secure part of the police station and emerged in to a well-lit reception area, with its view out on to the modern world that Jacky Fisher was now part of. A young man was seated in the waiting area. He was dressed in green trousers, a darker green pullover and a shirt with a matching tie. He stood up and walked towards them. Fisher noted he wore brown shoes that were highly polished. The man held a peaked cap in his left hand that Fisher would have recognised anywhere.

He proffered his hand to Fisher, and a firm handshake was exchanged by both men. The officer – Fisher recognised his rank as a captain – said, 'Hello, Staff Sergeant Fisher.'

Fisher stiffened to attention and said, 'Sir.'

'There no need for formalities Jacky, I'm Captain Beckman, I'm a military liaison officer. If you are genuinely from the 1940s, you won't know what that is. However, more of about that later. Miss Banning will be coming as your legal representative and for want of a better word, your chaperone. We are going to the barracks at Gillingham, where I am stationed. It's a Royal Engineers depot but we are the largest Army installation that can help you.'

The doors of the police station opened as they approached, causing Fisher to step backwards. Beckman smiled at Banning and shrugged his shoulders. Leaving the police station, they crossed to the officer's car.

Captain Beckman drove to the main London bound motorway and headed north. The traffic was light and Fisher spent the time looking out of the car's window at the Kent countryside as they sped along. They took the exit and soon pulled up at Brompton barracks. On the way Fisher looked at the proliferation of cars and dozens of giant trucks of all colours and sizes. It was a bright summer day with a clear blue sky. They overtook a truck finished in green with white lettering, and Fisher noted the number plate and the name were both distinctly German. He asked Beckman about it.

'We're friends with Germany now. They're our allies, although we still have troops in what was known as West Germany. I'm of German descent. My family moved to the United Kingdom before I was born. My great grandfather was in fact in the famous Afrika Korps.'

Fisher looked intrigued. 'With Rommel?'

'He was a mechanic, but he died when my dad was young. I'd have asked him if he knew Rommel though, if I could have done. It was the memory of my grandfather that inspired me to join the Army. We always had a photograph of him on our mantelpiece.

'Going back to what I was saying though, the Russian threat has subsided over the past decade, so no one's too sure how long they will be there. I'll be telling you more once we are at the barracks.'

The trio arrived at the army installation, the barrier was raised and, after parking his car, Captain Beckman showed them into the guard room. He filled out forms for the pair. The people behind the counter seemed to take no notice of Fisher and completed the mundane task without comment. Both Fisher and Trish Banning had their photographs taken. Jacky Fisher was amazed to see his likeness on the pass a few minutes later.

They left the guard room. He was given a lanyard with the pass attached which Pat Banning hung over Fisher's head. A soldier grounded the butt of his gun, a type which Fisher did not recognise, stood to attention and saluted the captain. The group re-entered the car and they drove a short distance to the captain's office. Once in the room,

Beckman opened a door and showed Jacky into a shower area. On a wooden chair were some army-green overalls with more fresh underwear and socks.

'You may wish to freshen up, there's shower gel and deodorant,' Fisher looked at the items. Beckman picked up the small black can, pushed the button spraying the perfumed mist, whilst raising his own arm. He showed Fisher how to access the shower gel and shampoo bottles snap lids.

Fisher nodded and Beckman left the room.

While Fisher set about his ablutions Beckman showed Trish Banning a print taken from an army microfiche, of one staff sergeant Jacky Fisher. Also there was a regimental photograph dating from before the war.

'It's undoubtedly him,' said Beckman, 'I'm having the original biked down from Catterick as we speak.'

'Why Catterick and are there still records dating back that far?'

'Catterick was where he was stationed and as to records? The easy answer is we have records dating back many years. All armed forces are photographed as a matter of course. They are not only for Mum's mantelpiece, but the main reason is we have a record of all our personnel. We've used these images even when identifying long-lost men unearthed from the remains in World War One trenches. This is done by facial measurements. So any unaccounted-for troops from those wars and any other conflicts can possibly be returned to their loved ones.'

Their conversation was halted by a knock on the door. An Asian man entered.

'Hello there, Doctor, oh do come on in, I've got a bit of a conundrum for you. He's just having a shower.'

'I've gathered that from your e-mail. What's your thoughts on him? It all seems a bit farfetched.'

'Just what I thought, in fact I was of a mind to humour him. I mean it's a darned good tale after all, but then—' Beckman turned his laptop's screen to allow the doctor a better view '—I've pasted a photo I took of him in roughly the same pose as the pre-war one,' Beckman adjusted the screen's colour adjustment and the modern picture turned to monochrome.

The Asian doctor looked at the photos. He asked Beckman to concentrate on the ears and expand the photo which Beckman did, he pressed a button on the laptop and a printer on a desk behind him chattered into life. Beckman handed the two prints to Singh.

'Whilst I was at medical school, I attended a lecture on the shapes of ears. Some time ago, you may have heard, a particular criminal case was proved. A would-be burglar was seen in silhouette by a neighbour, with his ear pressed to a window on a house across from his own. The neighbour called the police who apprehended the suspect a few roads away. Whilst the suspect pleaded innocence, scenes of crime officers lifted a print of his ear from the glass. He was convicted in, as I remember, a trial case, which drew on an ear science dating back many years.'

'I see what you mean. Now Fisher has told us he has a daughter born in 1939. We haven't checked yet as to whether she is still alive or if she had children. But could Jacky be one of her offspring? I personally have a cousin who looks for all the world like me, sure our dads are brothers, but we're not twins, and our mothers aren't at all related.'

'I can tell by the images of his ears that it's Jacky Fisher, and I can't explain it, Captain, but I'd bet my pension that he is the same man in the photograph. The only thing I had thought of was: could he have got in to the army's database and supplanted his picture?'

'Well I can't see it, Doctor, this was on a microfiche in army records; we still have the original as I told Miss Banning here, and it is being biked down from Yorkshire. That should be conclusive.'

Trish Banning spoke: 'I have to agree with you two that it seems Jacky Fisher is genuine.'

'OK, I'll just check him over when he's ready.' Doctor Singh tucked a stray hair under his turban.

'One thing, Doctor, Mr Fisher seemed to have a problem with two black detectives. I was told that he's unused to non-whites.'

'I'll bear that in mind, er, miss?'

'Pat Banning, I'm Mr Fisher's solicitor and I suppose as the captain said earlier, chaperone for want of a better word. He's a fascinating character and if all is to be believed...well, make your own mind up.'

Captain Beckman knocked on the shower room door and opened it. Jacky Fisher sat on the wooden chair pulling his trainers on.

'All done, Jacky? I've got our medic in to give you the once-over, then we'll be doing your debrief, will that be OK?'

'That's OK, sir.'

Fisher re-entered the room and his attention was immediately drawn to the Asian doctor. Fisher studied the man's face and the doctor's colourful turban.

Singh spoke first. 'Hello Jacky, my name is Doctor Singh. I'm told you are not used to Asian or black people. In this world it seems you have become part of, you will find many people from many countries living side by side. You may find my statement to be positive where other people may seem to be negative. The reason I can say that is because I am totally convinced you are genuine.'

Fisher looked up into the Asian man's eyes with an air of disbelief. 'Thank you, Doctor,' he said.

'I am able to tell you that, due to studies I have made, it is with this knowledge that I can personally authenticate your story. I'd like to examine you for and on behalf of the army; after all, it appears you are still a serving soldier.'

'Are you an army medic?' Fisher asked.

Singh looked at Captain Beckman who nodded out of Fisher's eye line.

'Yes I am. I look after the medical needs of all soldiers at these barracks. The army is different to your time, but I think Captain Beckman will tell you more much later on. Would you remove both your sweatshirt and T shirt please?' Singh opened his pilot's case and removed a stethoscope and a portable blood pressure machine.

Fisher complied. He tried not to flinch as the doctor moved towards him and placed the stethoscope's chest piece above his heart.

Singh asked Fisher to breathe deeply while listening through the earpieces. He looked into Fisher's eyes. 'You are a heavy smoker, Mr Fisher. You'll need to cut that down, and if you want to enjoy this world, quit altogether,' he said gravely. We have ways to help you give up, cut the craving, etcetera.' Singh had placed the Cossor from the blood pressure kit around Fisher's arm and began to inflate it. He put the chest piece of the stethoscope on Fisher's arm and slowly released the Cossor's pressure. Satisfied, he pulled the Velcro fastener from Fisher's arm. He made a note on Fisher's army record.

'Apart from the smoking you are in tip-top order. I notice you have your blood group tattooed on your inner arm.'

'It was given to all German army personnel.' Fisher looked away from the Asian doctor in case he knew the truth.

'Handy I'd say in time of war,' Singh replied, looking up at Fisher.

Fisher shrugged his shoulders.

Captain Beckman spoke. 'I've read up quite a bit about the "British Free Corps" on line—' he indicated the screen in front of him '—while you were showering. Was it your intention to use it as a ruse or plan to try to escape?'

'There was a plan involving me, Ernie Peters and a Welsh sailor called Evans. I can't remember or recall even if I knew his first name, but I know he was on a small warship, possibly a corvette which was torpedoed, he was the only survivor. The U boat picked him up and he joined the Kreigsmarine.'

Beckman said nothing as he tapped the keys on his laptop. 'Peters, Ernest, mmm there's quite a few, do you know where he hailed from?'

'He was from Rotherham, sir.'

'Oh yes got him, His last known whereabouts was a Stalag near Dallgow-Döberitz. Coincidently, that was your last known location too.'

'If you say so, sir, we were both recruited there.'

'Who by?' Beckman was tapping away on his laptop.

Fisher wondered if he was in trouble all these years, Williams was older than himself any way and from what Beckman had said, Fisher himself was over a hundred years old, 'I can't remember, I'll have to think about it.'

'OK, we'll go into that later; do you know where you did your training for the Waffen SS?' Fisher of course remembered it as if it were yesterday. The Russian prisoners Mr. Komatsu and the young Leutnant, the aide to the general. He wondered with Beckman's seemingly great knowledge of the time if he should be too precise in his memories.

'I'm afraid the German's weren't too keen on letting us know where we were. After all we were prisoners of war.'

Beckman looked up from the laptop. 'Oh yes, quite right, I'd forgotten that. The prisoners who worked for the Nazis, what did they do?'

'Oh, you mean the Arbeits-Kommandos. The work details?'

'If that's the correct term.'

'They cleared up bomb damage and did general labouring.'

'Were they paid?'

'Yes, also they were able to go to bars and buy tobacco and cigarettes; they were given extra food away from the camp.'

'Did you?'

'No I didn't agree with helping the enemy.'

Beckman looked up in surprise from his computer. 'But you joined the Waffen SS!'

Fisher shrugged his shoulders again. 'We were looking for a way out.'

'A way out of what exactly?' asked the young officer.

'Prison, being locked up for doing your job. It wasn't a crime to fight the Nazis. But the punishment for being caught, for not dying on the beach, was to be locked away.'

'You say you felt subjugated for being caught. Imprisoned for being a soldier.'

'How do you see it then, sir?'

Beckman paused for a second, rubbing his chin in thought.

'You're right of course. I'd never thought about it in that way before. As there are so few wars now, we don't think of POWs. Apart from those two airmen in Iraq, John Nichol and…' Beckman paused to remember.

'Wasn't it John Peters?' Singh suggested.

'Yep that was him.'

Fisher looked puzzled.

'Long story, Jacky,' Beckman said.

'Oh?' Fisher looked quizzically.

'We went to war with Iraq. One of our planes was shot down. The Iraqi dictator used the two airmen as pawns.'

Fisher remembered the bruised and battered airman on the railway station in Stettin, and some of the others he had seen after air raids. Their uniforms ragged and dirty. 'Only two!' He exclaimed.

'Planes are more difficult to shoot down now, Jacky.'

Fisher nodded, taking in the facts.

'We need to decide where you will fit in with us. I can guarantee you'll be checked over by doctors and scientists. We may accept you, but there'll be doubters and sceptics. Also, later today we'll fix you up with some accommodation; it won't be among the young lads, I wouldn't encumber you with them, not in your early days back in the army.'

Fisher smiled. 'The ones I've seen up to now seem good boys.'

'Trust me, that all changes when they've been on the town pubbing and clubbing,'

Fisher did not understand, but said nothing. As Beckman had promised, Fisher was allocated a single room with functional but basic furniture. The view over the army base probably had not altered much over the years, but the warm comfortable quarters were nothing like he had ever experienced in either the British Army, or the totalitarian Waffen SS of Adolf Hitler's war machine.

Chapter Eleven

In the Army—again

Jacky Fisher had a new change of clothes awaiting him when he was shown the room. Pat Banning and Beckman had accompanied him to the camp's restaurant and they ate their fill. The clothes consisted of a charcoal-grey pair of trousers, a white shirt hung over the back of a chair, with two more in cellophane wrappings nearby. Five pairs of new multi-coloured boxer shorts and a packet of socks were laid out on his bed. A black three-quarter length corduroy jacket on a wooden hanger hung from the room's door handle. Some lightweight slip-on shoes were positioned against the wall under the radiator. A blue and white sports bag was also laid on the bed. A young soldier who was in the corridor indicated the garments.

'There's some threads on the bed for ya, mate. Captain got them sent up for you.'

Fisher looked at the young black soldier. His accent pure Liverpudlian, he was, however, of Jamaican heritage. 'Thank you, but threads?' he asked, smiling. He still felt awkward in the presence of the black soldier.

'Threads, clothes, togs, you know. You seem a bit old for all this. What's your story, mate?'

'Everyone seems to ask the same thing.'

'There was a rumour about you that's all.'

'What was the rumour?'

'You're saying that you're like "The Terminator". You came forward through time.'

'Someone else mentioned that name before. I'm still not too sure what it means. What's a Terminator?'

'You gotta be having a laugh with us. You've never heard of The Terminator! I've got the DVD. Come along later, I'll show you. We can have a few beers with the lads.' He laughed out loud. 'I can't believe you've never heard of Arnie.'

'Staff Sergeant Fisher will have to decline your invitation, Private Galloway,' Captain Beckman interjected.

Galloway snapped to attention, 'Sir!'

'I'm not surprised though, Jacky. Walls, it seem, have ears.' He looked at the retreating figure of Private Galloway.

Fisher shrugged his shoulders.

'Today is Monday. I've gone as far as I can with you. You'll be going to London to meet the sceptics I told you about, but before then we may have a surprise for you. Your DNA – you won't know this but that's a term for a genetic fingerprint that is a unique to you as those on your hands – came back as positive. We went to the address you gave us in Chelmsford, your old house in fact, and to our great surprise we've found your daughter…'

'Hattie!' Fisher shouted, standing up. 'You've found my Hattie!'

'Yes, indeed we have. We were able to cross-match your DNA with her. There is news also of your wife, Victoria. She is alive and although a great age, in her late nineties in fact, she is fairly well, although according to Harriet suffering from dementia.'

'Is that serious?' asked Fisher. 'Oh my poor Queenie. What is this dem…?'

'She can often clearly remember things from many years ago, but not people she met recently, or something she did yesterday. As I said sometimes those memories of many years ago are thought of as yesterday.'

Fisher remembered his grandmother had the same condition. He told Beckman, 'My Granny went that way. My old mum just said Gran had gone soft in the head.'

'I know what you mean. In this modern world we call it Dementia or in severe cases Alzheimer's disease. We don't in this modern world mention "soft in the head", and that's along with "darkies" etc.'

Fisher nodded.

'I'll be handing you over to the auspices of The Royal Military Police.' Beckman saw the change in Fisher's face. 'Oh Jacky they aren't the bad guys they used to be in your time. They do police the Army of course, and the Army would be a poorer place for them, but their role has changed immeasurably. When you're dressed, square away you stuff in your sports bag and then come over to my office. It's unlikely you'll come back here. It's going to be the start of a great adventure.'

Fisher was sad to be leaving Beckman. He had cause to remember the RMPs in a bad light. He thought back to pre-war Catterick and the pile of bruised and bloodied squaddies after a boisterous night's dancing and perhaps when too many beers had been consumed, fighting either among themselves, or the locals. The hard faces of the ruthless military cops as they manhandled the hapless soldiers from the flat-back trucks, throwing them on to the tarmac outside the guard room.

Fisher dressed and ten minutes later, clutching the zipped holdall containing his meagre possessions, knocked at Beckman's door.

'Come in!' called the captain.

Fisher entered and his attention was immediately drawn to a pair of well-built men in matching charcoal blazers and lighter grey trousers. Both sported matching ties. The one who was sitting immediately stood and spoke to him.

'Good morning…and until we ascertain your status, if any, in the British Army, you will be referred to as Mister Fisher. Do you understand?'

Fisher nodded, feeling the sweat accumulating on his spine already. A feeling of dread hung like a cannon ball in his stomach.

'I'm Staff Sergeant Bill Denys. You can call me Bill or Staff depending on how you feel. This is—' he indicated to the other man '—Corporal Rhys Davis. He is known of course as Taffy.' The Welsh man nodded at Fisher. Now Mister Fisher, is it OK to call you Jacky, or would you prefer Jack?'

'Jacky,' Fisher replied.

'Jacky it is then. We're leaving Brompton Barracks and we will be travelling to Chelmsford by car. Do you have any needs? I understand you've had breakfast, but we can stop at the services if you need a cup of tea or the toilet.'

Captain Beckman walked forward and offered his hand to Jacky. 'Well, good luck, I hope our paths cross again, Jacky. Whatever the sceptics think when they question you—' he looked at the two RMP men '—I'm of the opinion you are genuine. So once again good luck.'

★

Bill and Taffy escorted Fisher to the car. It was a large silver saloon. Fisher noticed there was another Military Police officer, a young woman in uniform, in the driver's seat and that the engine was running.

Taffy opened the rear nearside door of the car and indicated Fisher should sit. Fisher felt the seat envelop him. Bill was already in the opposite seat and helped Fisher with his safety-belt while Taffy sat up front with the driver.

'This is Lance-corporal Helen Davis. Another Welsh export.'

The woman did not acknowledge Fisher. Fisher had noticed the three-pointed star of the Mercedes Company, and thought back to the day he had left the prison camp in the open-top staff car.

They left the barracks, having surrendered their passes and been signed out. Their car soon joined a busy dual carriageway. The young woman driver, who up till now had remained silent, said to the Staff Sergeant,

'I've put the post code in the sat-nav, Staff, but I won't turn it on until we get through the Dartford Tunnel.'

'That's OK,' Bill replied.

Fisher noted the female spoke with ease to her senior. That would not have done in Fisher's army.

They sat in silence as the car swept along the wide dual

carriageway, Jacky Fisher thought, with reckless abandon. True, just like the motorway earlier in the week, there were no turnings or crossroads after finding their way from the barracks onto the main dual carriageway. The last time he had seen roads like this was in Nazi Germany, when he and his fellow captives were driven in trucks from the railhead in Berlin to the camp outside the suburbs. That was in the long hot summer of 1942.

The woman police driver lazily held the wheel one-handed, the car appeared to change gear on its own. The silence amazed him, as did the coolness that exuded from the small grills set in the instrument area, which pushed the cool air to the rear of the car.

The Army had taught Jacky Fisher to drive, although his first experience, aged eleven, had been in his Uncle Cyril's Austin Ruby – when Cyril had been too drunk to stand. His uncle always called it a boneshaker, it reeked of both petrol and exhaust fumes.

When they all went for days out to Clacton and Southend-on-Sea from their home in Chelmsford, he well remembered these journeys fighting nausea from the fumes. Cyril would have the windows wound down but they still had to make regular stops for Jacky to be sick.

After Fisher's father died, Uncle Cyril, his mother's brother, became a father figure to him. Cyril had fought in the trenches in the Great War, and had been a victim of mustard gas. The consequence was that he retched thick yellow phlegm from his lungs until the day he died. The Ruby, which never helped Uncle Cyril's condition, was consigned to his uncle's garage thereafter. The Army's Humber saloon cars and open-top scouts that Jacky

Fisher obtained his driving permit in, were boneshakers too compared with this modern car. He progressed on to tanks and trucks at Catterick in Yorkshire.

Fisher was born 25th of January 1911. His father Albert Fisher named his son after the nation's hero Admiral Lord Jacky Fisher who was seventy years old on that very day. The First Sea Lord was credited with redesigning the British Navy in the early years of the twentieth century. He was responsible for the introduction of the Dreadnought battleship; fast and manoeuvrable, armed with four turrets, she could deliver a blistering broadside. The Dreadnought at a stroke made not only the vast majority of the Royal Navy's heavy ships, but also those of the rest of the navies around the world, redundant and obsolete.

Four years later, his father joined HMS *Vanguard*, one of Britain's Dreadnoughts, as one of many gunnery officers. He was present at the Battle of Jutland. The *Vanguard* fought well, receiving no damage and she had returned safely to the Grand Fleet anchorage at Scapa Flow. On the ninth of July, the *Vanguard* inexplicably exploded, taking Albert Fisher and over eight hundred of his fellow sailors to their deaths. Of the ship's company, which included a visiting commander from the Imperial Japanese Navy, only forty bodies were recovered. Albert Fisher's was not amongst them.

They journeyed on crossing the Thames via the Dartford Tunnel. Fisher was amazed at the engineering achievements. As they left the tunnel he looked out of the rear window at the QE2 Bridge. The car increased speed and he noticed from the road signs they had joined the A12 dual carriageway. After twenty minutes they left main road and began to motor through the lush Essex countryside. Soon the car slowed and Jacky Fisher peered between the front headrests and looked out of the windscreen. Taffy in the front seat turned and looked over his shoulder into his Fisher's eyes and spoke to him.

'This is the nursing home where the lady whom we...' He checked his sentence and then carried on: '...they think is your wife, resides.' He sounded sceptical, he had heard all about this strange man who claimed to come from the past. Fisher noted the look in his eyes and realised how few people believed him. Beckman, he felt, was one of the few on his side.

The residence was located in what had originally been small country house. The car glided along the drive, the only noise emitted a slight rumble through the tyres as it passed over the compacted pea-gravel drive. The car halted outside the house, the driver silenced the engine. The Army detective eased his muscular frame from the seat and opened the rear door of the car. Jacky Fisher pulled the unusually designed cap they had given him onto his head. It was made of some kind of mesh with a strange adjuster. He had earlier read the label: 'Made in China. One size fits all.' Fisher would have preferred a cloth 'cheese cutter', but none of the police officers knew what he meant.

'This way, Jacky,' said the one who had told Fisher to call him Colin, 'it's just through here.'

Jacky could not place the all-pervading smell that assaulted his senses as they entered the home, though urine and disinfectant could be detected. They signed in the visitors' book. Jackie once again marvelled at the pens that wrote with no ink blots.

A black nurse led them into a bedroom. Jacky felt uncomfortable yet again; he never failed to be amazed by the amount of "coloureds" he encountered in day-to-day life, although his mentors had admonished him for the use of such words.

As they entered, the old woman in the bed looked up and locked her eyes onto him, and in a shrill almost dove-like voice called, 'Jacky, my Jacky!'

Even after so many years had passed in her life, Jacky Fisher recognised her. 'Queenie! My darling, I'm back.' Pulling the cap from his head and throwing it down, he strode across the room, ignoring the older woman who sat beside his wife. He took Queenie's hand and turned to his police minders. 'My wife, Victoria Fisher.'

The woman who sat beside his wife studied him closely; tears suddenly cascaded from her eyes and across her age-lined cheeks. Jacky looked down at her as she pursed her lips to speak.

'Father, can it really be you?'

'Hattie. Is it you? My lovely little girl?'

Jacky Fisher turned to the police officers. 'My lovely wife and daughter!'

'Mum has been suffering from Alzheimer's. She hasn't spoken in months. It's truly a miracle.' Harriot spoke to the Police officers: 'This is my dad. No shadow of a doubt, definitely and for sure. I don't know how, what sort of magic has been performed, but this is my father.' She held up the silver-framed photographs and showed them to the officers.

Fisher took his tobacco tin from his pocket, ignoring the looks of protest from the staff who thought he was going to smoke. He produced the identical although slightly worn copies he had carried across Europe and on into this bright new world.

Jacky sat down by his wife and gently took the old lady's in his. He looked into her watery pale blue eyes and saw some recognition of him.

Harriet spoke: 'Mum never believed you were dead. I cannot say how you are here. I don't remember you too well before you went off. Of course you couldn't tell Mum where you were going but we found out from the Red Cross and we were able to send you things.'

'Dundee cake!' Jacky Fisher said through a throat almost choked with tears. 'You sent me a Dundee cake!'

Harriet suddenly exclaimed, 'Oh, Lord yes, that blooming Dundee cake! Mum had a store of nuts from before the war.' She looked at the RMPs. 'I can remember most of the things we sent like it was yesterday. Mum made us go without so that my dad would have stuff in the prison camp in Germany.'

Queenie suddenly started singing a melody no one recognised. She squeezed Jacky's hand and nodded to him. He picked up the tune and crouching down, took his wife in his arms, although she was still seated, as if they were dancing. She held him tight with her shrill voice singing a tune unknown to most of those present.

Harriet smiled. 'That was Mum's favourite tune. It came from a film Mum and Dad went to see before the war. She said it was played on the radio during the war years and every time she heard it she was reminded of Dad.'

Jacky released his wife and she sank back against the back of her chair, smiling with tears running down her cheeks.

'My Jacky, my Jacky,' she sobbed, 'I always said he wasn't dead. Always. I told my eldest brother Jim before 'e went. I told 'em all, I did.' She looked over at the RMP officers and her daughter.

Behind the gathered party the door opened, and the black nurse gently said, 'Your sons are waiting outside, Mrs Elland. We have a certain number of people per patient allowed. It's the rules, you understand.' She looked away sheepishly.

The RMP officers glanced and one and other. The one in charge said they would leave if Jacky felt they weren't needed.

'I'm only here if you need me,' Fisher said.

'Can't my dad stay with me tonight?' asked Harriet.

Fisher answered before the RMP men could. 'I'm still in the Army you know, my dear girl. They are looking after me. But I won't be far away that's for sure.' Fisher looked towards the RMP officers and they signalled their response by leaving Queenie's room.

As they left two other men entered. Both looked at Fisher with surprise. They had obviously been primed about his appearance. The first who appeared to be the elder moved towards Queenie and kissed her on the forehead.

'Hello Gran, who's this here then?'

The old lady looked up at him. 'Who are you?' She asked seemingly confused. 'What do mean, who's this? It's my Jacky who's come back from the war. Your granddad. Come back 'e 'as.' She smiled at Fisher and once again gently squeezed his hand.

The elder of the two men said, 'I'm Alan, your grandson. You know me, Gran.'

'I ain't got no bleedin' grandsons, never seen ya before.' She cackled and playfully pinched the man's arm, causing him to flinch.

The second man stepped forward. 'You've got two, Gran. I'm Jack and I've got two kids. You know you've got Poppy and Sandy, your great granddaughters.'

Harriet spoke to her sons. 'Alan, Jack. This is,' she paused fighting back her tears as emotion took hold of her voice, 'as sure as we can be, your granddad, my dad, Jacky Fisher.' She looked at Fisher. 'I named Alan after his grandfather on his dad's side. That is my late husband, Desmond's father.' She indicated the second man. 'This is my younger son. I called him Jacky after you. Although he's Jacky as I said, but he prefers Jack. He's a retired footballer.' She began to ramble on about her deceased husband but her son Alan took her in his arms until her tears subsided.

'Retired eh? You don't seem old enough. How old are you Jack?' Fisher asked.

Jack Elland looked sheepish. He ignored Fisher and looked towards his mother. 'Mum, I can't see this is my granddad. He's younger than me. What's going on, Mum?'

Sensing the awkwardness Jacky Fisher addressed Alan Elland. 'Er, what trade do you have, Alan?'

'I'm a car dealer, used cars that is. But as Jack says if you are our granddad why are you so young? I mean it's just plain spooky. I'm fifty-two for goodness sake, Jack, he's forty-eight.' He looked at his brother: 'Can you explain this, Jack? Cos, as sure as eggs is eggs, I bleedin' can't.'

Before Jack could answer Jacky spoke: 'Can I explain to you?'

They both looked at this strange man. ‘Give it your best shot!’ they both chorused.

Chapter Twelve

The New World

The next few weeks were something of a haze for Jacky Fisher. He visited Queenie every day at first, with either Jack or Alan driving him. Alan had a different car every day – these vehicles, his elder grandson explained, were from his car sales. The old lady now often failed to recognise her husband. He became very frustrated when he was so sure that she was maybe playing games with him.

The Army board of doctors passed him as fit and he was discharged from their employ. Before this he met dozens of officers and civilians who all asked questions pertaining to the time before the Army, his training at Catterick, the Churchill tank and how it was operated. He was taken to a working example and was ordered to drive it and name the controls. This he did faultlessly.

On a day out he was taken to a museum and with four experts he was put through the vagaries of the vehicle, this time a static vehicle. After seeing the tank he was shown scenes from the Dieppe raid and quizzed on the photos. He pointed out his LCT and was asked to name the tanks and the bulldozer. He was able to tell them about the Spitfire and the Focke-Wulf, giving the number on this plane. After a short while a man clicking keys at a computer nodded his approval.

'The FW 190, "black 5" was from JG26. The "Spit" he describes, where the pilot was rescued, was from Biggin Hill. He went on to survive the war and fly on afterwards as an airline captain with BOAC. Increased his tally of "Huns" too.'

More tests were conducted including a re-run of his DNA under laboratory conditions. Harriet was present too and tested. He was shown into a room with Jack Elland.

'We are satisfied that you are genuine, Mr Fisher. We have been in touch with a professor who specialises in the theory of parallel universes at the Massachusetts Institute of Technology. Or MIT for short. We would like you to go there and have some tests done. But that will be in the future. Until then be with your wife and other relatives. You are a fascinating case, Jacky.'

Fisher was also told they would work out a sum of back pay and deposit it into a bank account which they had set up. He had learned about the vagaries of cash machines and modern banking whilst in the convalescent home.

This was along with lectures about salient points of history between 1943 and the present day. Many of the old soldiers sat in and added their recollections to the general proceeding, telling anecdotes that often brought chaos to the lessons.

Pat Banning said farewell and returned to her

law practice in Dover. Jack Elland became his guide, chaperone and mentor. They visited his old house in Chelmsford, which had changed in many subtle ways. There were white plastic double-glazed windows all round, with a conservatory at the rear. Central heating radiators in every room plus a new bathroom suite complete with shower. And a recently fitted smart new kitchen.

He saw photos of Queenie and Hattie as his daughter had grown up over the years while he was absent. More albums of her wedding to Desmond and their honeymoon. There also later photos of his grandsons as they had grown. These had been transferred to disc. Jacky was able to view them on the television. There were more discs of all of Jack's games with his Premier league teams along with his early years at school plus local Saturday and Sunday league teams.

Harriet explained that she and Desmond had purchased the house when the laws were changed in the 1980s. Her mother continued to live with them as the boys grew up. Desmond, she told him, had died suddenly. This was soon after he retired from a career as the sports master at Fisher's old school. Hattie found him slumped at the end of the garden where he had a pond stocked with his beloved koi carp.

Jack now worked as a commentator and pundit for a satellite sports channel. He explained to Fisher how he had played for Newcastle in their youth and senior teams and had then been bought by Southampton. He was later injured and forced to retire when he was twenty-eight years old.

'Twenty eight!' Fisher had said, barely believing his grandson.

'You don't want to play on too late. I could have coached lower league teams, or maybe even talent scouted for the bigger ones. However, I was offered the job with the satellite sports channel.' He indicated the plush house with all the accoutrements of wealth. 'All of this came from football one way or another. I'm forty-eight now so I'm fourteen years older than you Jacky.' He stated laughing as he did so.

'When do you do your work? You say a satellite television station. I learned a bit about it in the convalescent home. The people have to pay extra to watch football?'

'Yes that's about it. The game is very big, the pay is bigger for everyone. The boot makers give you their boots and then pay you to wear them.' He tapped the vehicle's steering wheel, 'And this car comes from Range Rover. Each year I get a new one and as long as I'm seen driving it to the games and studios I'll carry on getting them. Not like it was in your day, eh Jacky?' He laughed, 'I'm sorry I still can't call you Granddad.'

Fisher was given a large room at his grandson's house in the north Essex village of Black Notley. It was en-suite with shower, bidet and bath. The room looked over the garden. He could see the large swimming pool which, although it was indoor, could, be he had been told quickly converted to outdoors when the sun shone.

He got to know his great grandchildren. Poppy and

Sandy. They were initially very distant towards him but soon became interested in his life up to now. They downloaded information from the internet and asked him about his time before the war and the raid on Dieppe and later his incarceration in Germany. They bought some DVDs on line and watched them with him, asking many questions about life in the camp. *The Great Escape* and *The Mackenzie Break* were two of their favourites. Their father had told them not to mention their great grandfather's fantastic tale but he knew they probably would.

Poppy was at college, but Sandy who was aged fourteen still attended school. Jack Elland's wife Suzanne was a tall willowy blonde in her mid-forties. She seemed a troubled soul and Fisher suspected she drank too much. In the mornings she would swim in the pool after using the apparatus in their gym room. Then she would sit in the sauna or steam room until her husband took their younger daughter to school. He then either went off to work or returned later to his study. There was a fridge in a poolside bar which was well stocked with bottles of beer and white wine. Situated near this bar was also a table and chairs. Suzanne would often sit there and read newspapers and magazines.

Poppy had her own small car and drove herself to college. Fisher tried to engage Suzanne in conversation but she seemed more intent on the smart phone screen, tapping at it almost constantly. She would vaguely answer his enquiries with a distant look in her eyes. Fisher asked his grandson about Suzanne but he just brushed it away. He told Jacky that modern living brought modern problems and left it at that.

The family had a Springer Spaniel called Max. Fisher took the animal for long walks in the surrounding lush countryside. Deep in his mind, Fisher had questions he could not answer. He found a country pub on his travels and spent some time deep in thought, over half-pints of bitter. The pub had copies of daily newspapers and Jacky would read them while Max snoozed patiently at his feet.

*

On the next Saturday afternoon Jack took his grandfather to watch football at White Hart Lane. Spurs were playing Chelsea so it was a keenly contested match. They travelled in his black Range Rover and Fisher noted how he skilfully steered the large vehicle through the throngs of supporters, each decked out in their chosen team's replica shirts. A security man saw Jack Elland's car approaching and opened a gate allowing them in. Another man moved a traffic cone and ushered the large car into his reserved parking space.

Jacky Fisher watched the game from the television station's luxurious private box. A huge television set gave close-ups of the play. He declined the offer of what seemed to him to be an avalanche of food after eating an adequate portion. He later explained to Jack that for the last few years both in the POW camp and latterly in the Waffen SS, he often went hungry. Seeing the amount of food and exotic fruits which would seemingly be wasted worried Fisher. Jack shrugged and told him it was a sign of the times but the film crew and the caterers would make sure not too much if any went to waste.

Fisher and Elland were about to leave the stadium when

a portly Scotsman approached. Jack Elland introduced Jacky as he usually did as a family friend.

'I heard this here fellow is supposed to be yer fecking grandfather! How old are you then, mate?' He jabbed Fisher in the chest. 'Thirty, maybe thirty-five?'

Elland rounded on the man. 'Mind your own business, Jock!'

'It is my business. I've maybe got a scoop here. Did someone find the font of eternal youth, eh maybe? I'm saying you're a fraud friend, a fecking fraud.'

The man's attitude offended Fisher. He thought of his MP40. He would have cut this fat slobbering Scot down without a second's thought. Elland's voice snapped him back to reality.

'Come on, Jacky, let's get out of here!' Elland said guiding Fisher away.

'Who was that?' Fisher asked.

'Well he's a gutter press reporter. He's looking for any filth he can find out about anyone and anything. Who's bonking who, if anyone is on the take? Is some person living a lie? That sort of thing. It seems someone has blabbed. Jock Wolf he calls himself. He's got a column in one of the red mastheads. *Wolf's Cry*.'

'Bonking and living a lie?' Fisher asked.

Elland paused for a step and regarded his grandfather. 'Sleeping with someone you're not married to, that includes a person of the same sex! Living a lie, well appearing to be one thing when you are another.'

'I see, well that is, I think I do,' said Fisher.

'It's a whole different ball game these days, Jacky, in more ways than you'd think.'

After the encounter the pair retraced their steps the Range Rover. They travelled to the television station's studios where the day's games across the nation were picked over and the best goals that were scored shown from different angles, often in slow motion.

Fisher watched the programme in a viewing room with some people he did not recognise, but who took him on board with the explanation that he was Jack Elland's friend. After the programme, although it was late, when they left the television studios Jacky asked his grandson if they were far from St John's Wood.

'Not that far. No cricket there, Jacky, this time of year.'

'I need to look at a house, I have the address.' He didn't enlarge, but told Jack Elland the location.

To Fisher's surprise his grandson pushed a button on the dash of his Ranger Rover and a small illuminated screen was revealed. 'I suppose you don't have the post-code?' He laughed, but didn't wait for a response. He touched the screen several times and entered the address.

A woman's voice spoke softly and soon began to direct his grandson along the streets of north London. Jack pointed out Lord's cricket ground as they passed. He told his grandfather that when he had been selected to play for the English national football side, he had participated in a charity match with the England cricket team, first cricket, then football.

'Did you play for England then?' Jacky Fisher asked.

'Nah, I got crocked with a bad ham-string strain and I was out for six months, so I missed the selection.'

'In my day they played through that sort of injury,' Jacky said.

'Not anymore,' Elland laughed. 'Oh here we are.' The voice in the sat-nav had alerted the pair to their arrival. 'Do you know who lives here then?'

'Er, no it's an address that's in my mind, that's all.'

Jack Elland looked across the Range Rover's spacious cabin at his grandfather with suspicious eyes. 'An address, that's *JUST* in your mind? Come on, Jacky, you can do better than that.'

'I can't explain why I know it or how. We had a meeting with a nasty sort of person from the German secret service. It was called the Abwehr.'

'When was this?'

'In time, actually only about a few months ago, but in reality it was June 1943.'

'So he asked you to do what?'

'They were going to arrange for three of us to escape via Sweden.

'Why an earth would they allow that? Surely you knew things that could be useful to us, by that I mean the British.'

'To get in touch with an agent they had lost contact with.'

Elland thought for a few seconds. 'And he lived here?' Jack Elland indicated the large house they were parked outside of.

'They didn't say if it was a he or a she. They said the agent was close to Winston Churchill.'

Elland blew his cheeks out in surprise. 'I wasn't too up on history apart from what our mum told us about you, but a Nazi agent in Churchill's—what would that be—his cabinet? How would you know who it was?'

'The thing is, if we had escaped, we would, like any, or all successful "home runs" as they were called, have met Winston Churchill. It was a tradition, you see. I'm not too sure if we may have rubbed shoulders with others in government. I don't know, it's all very vague. Perhaps the agent would have known about us...but I don't know. As far as I can say, I feel we didn't get the full instructions. Then as you know it all went wrong and I ended up here.'

'You've told us why you joined the...what was it again?'

'Waffen SS.'

'OK. Was it as you say a way of getting out of prison, or was there anything else?'

Fisher was about to reply when the inside of the car was illuminated by flashing lights and a police siren momentarily sounded. Jack Elland switched of the engine and opened the driver's side window. Jacky could hear the distorted voices from a police radio. An officer in a day-glow jacket appeared beside the former football star and shone a torch in Jack's face.

'Good evening, Mister Elland.' He paused and called back to the patrol car, 'All in order, it's Jack Elland all right.' He turned his gaze to Fisher: 'Can I ask who are you, sir?'

Jack Elland spoke first. 'This is a relative of mine, Jacky Fisher.'

'Good evening, sir. Can I ask why you gentlemen are parked here?'

Jack Elland spoke. 'We pulled up for a chat. Any problem there, Officer?'

Jacky Fisher was aware that another policeman had appeared by his door. Elland activated the passenger-side window and it slid noiselessly down. The newcomer spoke with a Newcastle accent.

'Well hello there, Jacky Elland! I used to watch you with my dad when I was growing up, when you played for Newcastle United that is.'

Elland smiled, 'I'm glad you were a fan. Toon Army?'

'Aye ya right I was. All my family too. Mam, Dad, brothers. It's an honour to meet you, it is really. We were all sorry when you signed for Southampton. Proper cut-up my dad was, like.'

'The Toons sold me, nothing much I could do,' Elland said with irony in his voice, 'except bank the money.' Elland laughed again but then turned to the first officer. 'Anyway if that's all we'll be pushing off. What made you stop, by the way?'

'We had a call about your car outside this house.' The police officer nodded towards the impressive mansion. They're Russkies who live here. They're a pretty nervous bunch.'

'They must be a new lot in then? It's the main road after all. Do they call if anyone parks here? Free world and all that!' Elland exclaimed.

'They've been here a good few years now as far as I know. They are Oligarchs if that's the right term. It used to be one of the aristocracy until a few years ago that lived here'

'Anyone we'd know?'

'Can't say I remember now, anyway you can make your way home now. Goodnight, Mr Elland, Mr Fisher.'

★

After breakfast next day Jack Elland took Fisher into what he called his "Lad's Room". Apart from an apparently well stocked bar, an eight-ball pool and snooker table, there was several life-sized blown-up action photos of Jack Elland in his Newcastle United strip. In the corner was a large desk with six computer screens affixed to a large tubular steel bracket screwed directly into the ceiling. Jack clicked a mouse and bought the screens to life.

'Sit yourself down, Jacky.' Elland indicated a spare chair. He pointed to the screens naming each as his went, 'Facebook, Twitter, Instagram. News feeds, Sky and BBC news channels, plus all the satellite sports.' He turned and smiled at Fisher before clicking on to the large main screen. 'Now let's have a look.' He tapped in the address Jacky had given him the previous evening. 'OK, now from before the war and up until 1988 it was occupied by this family.' He pointed the name out to Jacky: 'Do they mean anything to you?'

'No, nothing I'm afraid. Is there any more?' Fisher shrugged his shoulders.

Elland opened other pages, searching back as he did so. He whistled softly as an old newspaper page filled the screen. 'There was a report that two of the family were killed in late 1942. The husband and wife. They were in a small theatre in the area near Shaftsbury Avenue when a stick of bombs hit. The whole place was flattened.' He leaned forward and scrolled the page down. 'It says there was a crush getting to the theatre's basement shelter. A dozen died. A few bodies were found, though not theirs.' He used the mouse to point to the pertinent names, he deftly highlighted them and left the page. He brought up an on-line encyclopaedia and pasted in the names.

'What else have you found out?' Fisher asked.

'Well it says here that the human remains weren't found until repairs were started in the early fifties when the site was being excavated. They were then all identified from their ID cards, jewellery, clothing, that sort of thing. Up to then no one knew of their fate. I expect that's why the Nazis were in the dark.

'Theatres, Jacky, were way down the list of bomb damage to be repaired. Industry and housing came first. It says that the woman was French. They married before the war, oh it says here she was Jewish. Now I wonder.' He scrolled the page down: 'Yes, her family were deported to a camp somewhere in Germany when the Nazis over-ran France. The husband though, he was aristocratic, prep school, Eton, Oxford, Coldstream Guards, the whole nine yards.' Elland looked further down the page. 'He spent most of the First World war at Windsor, yep all the usual guff. However, she wasn't close to the war cabinet. But he was! One of the Prime Minister's closest aides. If the agent were either, I'd say it was him. Perhaps they were being blackmailed by the Germans to keep her family alive?'

'Does it say if they survived?'

'It doesn't even name them, I'm sorry to say, Jacky. I expect we could get the authorities to trace their fate but would it do any good?'

Fisher looked down at the floor and shook his head. 'I don't suppose it would,' he said sadly.

Chapter Thirteen

The need to reveal and make amends

Fisher was awoken a few days later by the shrill voice of his great-grand daughter Poppy, calling out to her father. 'Dad, Dad quick. There's loads of reporters outside, TV cameras the lot!'

From the hallway came the noise of the gate phone being constantly buzzed and distorted voices clamouring for attention.

Jack Elland came into Fisher's room and looked out of the window. He sighed and pulled the curtains across, dropping the Venetian blind as he did so. 'Stay away from the windows, Jacky. We're surrounded by the press. The bastards are looking over the back fence. The paparazzi will have their long lenses out. This has Jock Wolf's name all over it.'

'What are they after?' Fisher asked.

'You probably!' retorted Elland.

'Can't you call the police?'

'They're as effective these days, Jacky, as a chocolate teapot. I'll go out and see the reporters and see what they want.' As he spoke his mobile phone sounded. 'Hello, OK, yes, but just you though. No one else!' He turned to his grandfather: 'There's a news team from my television station. I know them all so they won't twist our words, well I hope not. I've said just the girl, Marianne Colburg, can come in, she's only young but she always seems to be genuine and honest.'

★

Later Jacky Fisher and Jack Elland sat in the retired footballer's well-appointed living room. Jack had stipulated no camera or recording device, only a notebook. Fisher began his tale editing out some of the more gory facts. As the scenario unfolded the young woman reporter's face grew tense.

Eventually she spoke. 'I can't claim to be an expert on the Second World War. Far from it. In fact apart from watching endless re-runs of both *The Great Escape* and *The Colditz Story* on television and DVD with my granddad, there's not much I can say about it all. Sure in school we covered, no, barely covered the causes of the First and Second World Wars, the Korean War, even the Vietnam conflict, but I think even our tutors didn't have a clue. We didn't get told as far as I know about—' she consulted her notes '—Dieppe? I wish my grandfather was still alive. He'd know all about it. Of course with your granddad here, Jack, you're that much better off than me.'

Elland's phone sounded again and he keyed the device and spoke briefly. He went to the main entrance door opened it and looked at the electronically operated gates. All along the eight-foot-high front walls cameramen snapped away, flash guns illuminating like super nova stars even in the bright sunlight, other pressmen alerted to activity appeared along the wall as if by magic. He guessed they would all be standing on their aluminium stepladders. He took a remote control from his pocket and activated the device, so unlocking the smaller side gate. This was pushed open and two men, after struggling with some newsmen, entered. They firmly closed the gate behind them and hurriedly made their way up the drive. Elland waited as they approached. He already knew they were Ministry of Defence men.

He showed them into the living room. As he made to follow he glanced at Suzanne sitting alone, as usual, in the wood-panelled dining room, demurely eating a sandwich accompanied by a tall glass of white wine. Their eyes met briefly. He knew he should try to help her but the events surrounding the appearance of Jacky Fisher clouded his reasoning. She had been at his side always during his playing career, his various injuries and then moving away from her friends from the north-east to the south of England. He bought them a luxurious house in a gated community near the New Forest, but the isolation weighed heavily on her.

As he entered the living room the two MOD men had seated themselves on one of the sofas. 'My name is Willis and this is Captain Planer.' Major Willis pointed at the reporter. 'Just how much have you told this young lady?'

'About all, everything that is.'

'That wasn't wise. Young lady, this is a subject of national importance, I will need to take your notebook.' Ignoring the shocked look from the woman, he continued,

'But after I have taken advice from my superiors and *if* they do decide to go public, your notes and the scoop that you've been given will be all yours.

'Can you do that?' she exploded.

'The short answer is yes. If necessary we can have you taken into custody and your organisation issued with a "D" notice. It is that serious. Do we have an understanding?'

She nodded. 'What will I tell my boss?'

'We have ways and means to let your boss know.'

Elland asked, 'Do we keep Jacky here?'

Major Willis stood and indicated to Elland and Planer to follow him to the hallway. 'I think that's off the agenda now,' he said quietly so Marianne Colburg would not hear. 'How about you take your big black car for a nice little ride and hopefully the press will follow you; we'll take Jacky back to London in our people carrier.'

Marianne Colburg re-joined the throng of reporters after being let out of the side gate by the family's gardener. They clamoured for a story from her but as agreed with Jack Elland she remained tight lipped. Two police cars then arrived and the crews amounting to four officers cleared the newsmen from the gates which then slowly opened.

One of the sections of garage door noiselessly rolled up and Jack Elland's black Range Rover emerged from its lair in the five car garage. He drove slowly down his driveway and out of his property ignoring the clamour of microphone-holding press corps and sped away, the reporters risking their lives flashing their cameras through the black privacy windows at the figure huddled on the back seat. Some of the paparazzi had motorbikes and were able to set off quickly after the big car and soon outpaced it. When he had put some distance between his property and them, he called to his house keeper to come out from under the covers.

While he was taking the newsmen on a scenic tour of Essex, Willis and Planer retrieved their vehicle from the roadway outside Elland's mansion and secreted Fisher away to London.

Jack Elland caught up with his grandfather later that week at a retired serviceman's club in southeast London. Fisher had spent some time here learning about the new world he was part of some weeks earlier. Major Willis had smoothed the path for such an apparently young man to be billeted in one of their guest rooms. He had become a minor celebrity there as he reminisced with other old soldiers gathered there.

They in their turn told him of fighting in Korea, Aden and Northern Ireland. Jacky realised then that very few people could back his story up. Beckman had mentioned some veterans of the Dieppe raid. Even the very youngest would now have been in their nineties and Beckman said they were unsure if he were able to meet with them. The young soldiers on the Dieppe raid were mainly Canadians.

'What have they worked out?' Jack Elland asked his grandfather. 'The press seem to have gone to ground on the matter. But I don't think it's gone away. There's a lot going on in the news at the moment so it will be on the back burner.'

'The Major says we will be having a press conference later this month. He says there's too much on the internet to let it fade away.'

'You mean come clean about your arrival in our time?

Having to re-prove the DNA with our mum again. She's not young, Jacky, you seem to forget that. Not that little girl you left to go off to war. No, I can't see that working. You'll be a worldwide phenomenon. How about those people that you told me about. The ones you saw murdered in the barracks? Their families if they are still alive in Germany, even those as far away as Russia will surely want answers. They won't believe you and your mates did those deeds under orders. Do you know there are ninety-year-old concentration camp accountants being tried for mass murder, even though they claim nothing more than just to have done the soldiers' wages! Because they wore the uniform of the SS.'

'Those things were only for your ears, it wouldn't be wise to make them too well known. That's why I didn't tell your reporter friend.'

'What things are for only your grandson's ears?' Major Willis interrupted the conversation as he strode into the room.

'It doesn't matter, Major, just something my grandfather and I spoke about some time ago. I looked up this Waffen SS and saw the terrible things some of them did.'

Major Willis creased his brow when he spoke to Jack Elland. 'Jack, all armies in time of war do terrible things to their enemy. I have knowledge of soldiers in the British Army even today who have slaughtered prisoners in Iraq, Afghanistan and even as long ago as the so called "Troubles" in Northern Ireland. I was a second Lieutenant then. Some IRA, Provos as they were called, you may remember, were setting up an ambush for some poor bloody farmer because he wouldn't play their game. When we nabbed them they knew we wouldn't be able to prove it. Cocky load of Paddy bastards. So we had a quick conflab and it was agreed between us. We, as they say in the army, "slotted" them. Summary justice. Used their own guns too. No one could prove anything. So Mr Elland, we knew what went on with your grandfather and we will let those sleeping dogs get some rest.

'Jacky will stay here for the next week or. We are organising a rented house. We've decided on Kent, maybe the Dartford or Gravesend areas. This will make it easier for you to visit Hattie and Queenie. Jack and Alan will be just a short trip away. My bosses have formulated a press release. We will gloss over the Waffen SS episode as far as we can. As Jacky has said the main reason was to escape. We will stand or fall on that presumption. Do I make myself clear Jacky?' He smiled and gently said, 'it's for the best Jacky. We can still spirit you off to see Queenie as we can let Jack or Alan drive Hattie to wherever we billet you. The press release will go out in the next week or so. I hope that will quell the internet chatter.'

Fisher looked forlornly at his grandson. 'It seems I'll be like a sideshow exhibit.' He remembered seeing a two headed lady, he tried to remember whether it was at the Kursaal amusement park in Southend-on-Sea in Essex, or when his mother and uncle had ventured as far as Margate on the pleasure cruises they often went on.

'It'll be OK, Jacky. You really are a phenomenon though and as such you, or we need to milk it as much as possible. As you know after I retired from soccer I went to university studied for a degree and graduated in journalism. I could write your story. The back pay you got from the

Army won't last forever and I know you've got a payment of goodness knows how much of your old age pension coming, but you're still a young man. I've got as much money as any person could want but—' Elland smiled at his grandfather '—you need to put some away for any rainy days that come along. Hell, you never know there could be a film even. It won't be that bad, Jacky, you'll see.'

★

Major Willis suggested that Jacky grew a beard. Fisher often needed to shave twice a day as he such a prodigious hair growth. His hair was to be styled by a visiting hairdresser who would know nothing of his history. Also, although Jacky had perfect vision, some plain lensed, tinted glasses would further help him to blend in. It was agreed that he could visit cinemas and places of interest in the company of a police officer. It was agreed that it would be a woman and of roughly Fisher's age. It was further agreed that they would appear to be a couple.

Fisher felt that his marriage to Queenie was still very much a part of his reason to live, but in her mind she was in a place of her own now. On his last visit with Alan and Harriot she showed no comprehension of their presence. She sat looking out of the window, endlessly, softly humming a tune and occasionally mouthing soundless words.

Chapter Fourteen

Part-time wife

Fisher and his grandsons, Alan and Jack Elland, stood as a tall attractive woman entered the room in the armed forces veterans' home. She was accompanied by Captain Planer. Fisher knew she was to be his "Minder", as Alan and Jack had dubbed her.

'She'll be eighteen stone with a beard and moustache – better than the one you're growing, Jacky!' Alan had chided him earlier that day.

'With muscles like a Russian shot putter. Like the ones who had to have their gender checked at the Olympics that time.' Jack Elland joined in the banter.

The woman introduced herself as Lizzy Goldman. She approached Fisher who went to shake her hand. She took his proffered hand, but pulled him towards her, kissing his cheek lightly. Fisher was surprised at her forwardness, but inhaled her perfumed womanly essence. He felt an unusual stirring in his loins. She noted his surprised look.

'Well I'm supposed to be your "part-time wife", as my brief from the Captain here states.' She nodded towards

Planer. 'I've been studying your case and so I'm fairly up to speed.' She looked at the small suitcase and sports bag. He had retained the bag from his time at Brompton barracks. 'Now I see you've packed, so we'll be leaving here soon. If you like to make your farewells, we'll be off. You won't be far away from your grandsons. In fact we'll be having something of a house-warming "do" once we've moved in, to make it look natural, to our neighbours, if you know what I mean?'

Jack offered his hand and pulled his grandfather towards him, hugging Fisher close to his body. Alan stepped forward as his brother released his bear hug and did the same. 'I still can't see you as, or call you Grandad. We never had you in the past when we were growing up, we didn't have either your presence or your wisdom to get us along. But, Jack myself and the rest of the family have bought you a little something.' He passed over a small but brightly coloured bag; 'It will remind you of your time—' he paused searching for the right words '—I suppose...I mean your time in our time. Does that make sense?'

Fisher opened the bag. He retrieved an envelope which contained a greetings card wishing him luck and a white cardboard cube measuring about three inches. He opened it and found it to be an electronic watch. It showed the time, date and year on an LCD screen. The seconds ticked relentlessly on.

'I don't know what to say...' He beamed at the gathered throng of his relatives and those he now considered to be friends. 'It must have cost a small fortune.' He checked it again, marvelling at the watch, encased in such a small black plastic case.

'Well the technology is very cheap nowadays. If fact when the battery dies you can just throw it in the bin. Damn clever, these Japanese. It has a light but, don't use it too much or the battery will run down.'

Fisher placed the watch on his left wrist and fastened the strap. 'I won't. Thank you all once again.'

He looked up and saw that Lizzie was holding his zipper jacket over her crooked arm with his holdall and suitcase in each hand. 'All ready?' she enquired.

Fisher was fully aware she wanted to be gone. He smiled at the assembled party and followed Lizzie from the room.

After putting his baggage away in the boot of the smart red Lexus saloon car, he settled in for the journey. Fisher asked Lizzie their destination.

'Swanley, it's in north Kent.'

'Why Swanley?'

'Well it's alongside the M25, close to the Dartford River Crossing, so we can visit Queenie, your daughter and your grandsons. Also the M20 runs equally close by, so we can go on days out, Maidstone let's say, or down to the coast, Folkestone or Hastings. So you ask why Swanley? It's suburbia. Anonymous estates where people trundle off to London each day, wash their cars or cut their lawns on a Sunday. No one will need to know who you are.'

'Do you go to work?'

'At the present time you are my work. I'm on light duties after a mishap with my main job.'

'Which is? I thought you were a policewoman.'

'We're known as police officers these days. I'm on close protection duties. That means we can be bodyguards for anyone from the Prime Minister, other key politicians, even members of the Royal Family.'

'You've met the Prime Minister. What's he like?'

'Well he's a she. Clare Martin. She's forty. Very nice lady. She's only slightly built, but a real firebrand in Parliament. She doesn't suffer fools I can tell you. We have to watch our step with her.'

'Clare? It doesn't sound like a prime minister's name and only forty? You say you had a mishap?'

'I shouldn't really divulge it but, we were escorting a foreign diplomat's car. Our vehicle was slowed by a large tipper truck making a wide left turn into a side road. It was baulked by a car emerging from that same road. Our driver smelled a rat and thinking it was a hijack attempt, he hit the fast peddle and tried to overtake the tipper, just as this other car emerged. We smacked into it and were bounced into parked vehicles while travelling about sixty miles per hour. I sustained a broken arm and wrist—' she waved her left arm towards him, articulating the joint '—when the air bag deployed. The police driver who also wasn't wearing a seat belt got crushed ribs and facial injuries from his air bag going off. Mine is almost healed but it's still weak. Hence the light duties.'

'Oh,' Fisher said, tapping the car's dash to his fore where this car's safety feature lay hidden; 'I was told these things were supposed to save injury.'

'Only if the seat belts are worn. In our sort of work where we may have to exit the car, draw weapons and so on, you cannot be constrained by seat belts.'

'Weapons? So you're an armed—' he paused '—police officer then? You have guns?'

'Glock pistol. Also when needed, a machine pistol, that's usually the Heckler and Koch. Also a stunning device called a Taser.'

'What's that?'

'It's a small weapon, it fits nicely in the hand. A compressed nitrogen cylinder shoots out two tungsten barbs which penetrate the perpetrator's flesh, even penetrates medium to heavy clothing. They are connected to the weapon by thin wires. A charge of many thousands of volts incapacitates the target. In short they hit the ground like a felled tree.'

'Are they killed?'

'No, there's no amperage. If you remember your physics lessons at school, it's the amps that kill, not the volts. There have been a few deaths with people with bad hearts, but not in this country. It happens if the criminal has a weak heart, or when the barbs strike the neck or head.'

The car's satellite navigation voice, which had been up to now fairly silent, instructed Lizzie on an upcoming junction.

'Not far now,' she said, turning off the dual carriageway. 'There's a pub coming up in about a mile on the left. I'm sure it does pub grub. Do you want to stop? I don't know what there'll be at the house by way of food. If it was a "safe house" it will normally be well provisioned. But I'll see when we get there. We'll also need to do a supermarket shop soon anyway.' She guided the car into the car parking area.

★

Fisher and Lizzie Goldman finished their food. Jacky had

consumed a half pint of best bitter beer with his meal. Lizzie remarked that not many men drank bitter these days and then not in half pints.

'A half does me. I don't want to get bloated. I do miss a smoke after though.' He tapped his left side upper arm, 'but since these I got these patches I've not wanted to smoke, I can just remember having a roll-up after a meal. I suspect it was these anti-smoking patches gave me such really bad nightmares.' He was silent and reflected the terrible dreams while "under" from the effects of anaesthetic at the dental surgery before joining his detail in the Waffen SS.

'I must say though, you are very trim, Jacky.' She looked at him appreciatively. 'Now you're thirty-two aren't you? Two years younger than me,' she laughed, 'even though you were born in 1911.' She continued, 'I'm in the gym most mornings before work, it's just a short walk from my flat, then jump on the Underground to the office. I fight to keep my weight level and the flab from my tummy. Too much booze after work though undoes my efforts.'

'You're not married then? Fisher asked.

'I was in a long-term relationship with another copper, but it didn't work out. Different shifts, then time away with the "Job". He found someone else. Still, as I said I'm your part-time wife for the next few months, until they sort out what to do with you that is.'

After leaving the pub the sat-nav guided them onward to their rented house. Lizzie parked the Lexus on the drive of a smart chalet bungalow. Fisher noted the grass needed cutting and mentioned it to Lizzie.

'I'll check if there's a Flymo in the shed. The owner

of the house is working abroad for two years. The place comes with all the mod-cons.' She took some keys from her shoulder bag: 'Let's go in and have a gander.'

'Flymo?'

'Lawn mower,' Lizzie said as she opened the door. The house smelt musty, but after they opened all the windows the air soon cleared. She emptied the electric kettle and refilled it. 'Tea or coffee,' she asked.

'Oh, tea most definitely, with milk and two sugars,' Fisher emphasised, remembering the Ersatz version back in Nazi Germany.

'I'm strictly a caffeine gal,' she said 'I don't start firing on all cylinders until I'm on mug number three in the mornings. But you should cut down on the sugar. It won't do that figure of yours any good!'

Fisher explained his aversion to coffee.

'That sounds really gross! Roasted and ground acorns? Yuck!'

After their hot drinks they explored the house. There was an en-suite shower in the back bedroom. Fisher gave this room to Lizzie. He still had an ingrained hatred of showers from his time at school, in the British Army and latterly in the training barracks in Germany. He told Lizzie about this too.

A look outside on the rear garden's patio revealed a large hot tub. Lizzie consulted the instructions and switched it on. She tested the water after lifting the insulated cover and discovered the water was still relatively warm.

They got in the car and retraced their route to the main town, stopping in the supermarket's ample parking area. They grabbed a trolley and bought several meals worth of shopping, tea, coffee plus some vegetables and frozen oven chips. Fisher had his debit and credit cards ready and paid for their goods at the checkout.

As they drove home they passed several restaurants. Lizzie asked him if he like Chinese or Indian food.

'I've never tried,' he admitted, 'perhaps you can help me?'

'Well for tonight we have steak and the oven chips. Do you barbecue?'

'I've seen them doing it when I…well when I arrived in France. Of course we were taught to live off the land in—' he paused again '—the Waffen SS. Trapping rabbits, birds and other small creatures. One of the other squads caught and killed a wild boar and set about roasting it over an open fire. They all ended up in the medical centre. I was told at the time they hadn't cooked it properly.'

'That's the trouble with pork.' Lizzie grimaced at the thought of the badly cooked meat.

Later that evening the sinking sun turned the blue sky dark cobalt. Lizzie had prepared an excellent meal as promised. They had already drunk several glasses of wine and were sitting in the hot tub. With the warming water bubbling about them, he spoke about his life. She told him about her strict upbringing in a north London Jewish family. He told her about his father and mother. How he recalled the Dieppe raid and the hundreds of slain young Canadians, the prison camp, training, his time in Stettin and his propulsion into this modern time.

Neither of them possessed any swimming attire so

Fisher wore a pair of his coloured boxer shorts and Lizzie a skimpy bra and panties. The tub had its own sound system with sound activated lights. Lizzie plugged her MP3 player into the unit and they listened to several albums by "Above and Beyond".

Slightly tipsy, she told him she needed to use the loo. Standing on wobbly legs she suddenly slipped and fell into Fisher's arm. With her mouth less than an inch from his, she thrust forward her tongue searching his mouth. She suddenly straddled his groin with hers, grinding her pubic area against his hardening manhood. She shivered once as she quickly reached a shattering climax.

'Phew, that's been a long time coming,' she told him once again, scouring his mouth with her tongue.

Fisher reached under the water and pulled his shorts down and at the same time pulled the flimsy panties from her body. Fully aroused now, as he thrust into her soft warm sex, he felt the pent-up frustrations of the years evaporate. He picked her up, muscles honed iron-hard by the Nazi terror regime. He effortlessly turned her body. Fisher was standing now, the water swirling around his knees. She gripped his waist with her long legs as his orgasm approached. She kissed him deeply again and she felt his hot semen flood into her.

As they felt their orgasms fade away, Fisher looked up at the nearby windows and said, 'I hope no one was watching!'

Lizzie kissed him deeply and gasped, 'Do you know, I don't give a shit!'

They dried off and went inside the house. She poured the last of the wine, expertly dividing the liquid equally.

Fisher pulled the curtains across and gently refused the proffered wine. He took the glasses and placed them on coffee table. He turned and gently pulled her down on the sofa. This time he gently made love to her and once again they both orgasmed together.

Lizzie lay back on the soft cushioned settee and smiled at Fisher. 'Tell you what, you're definitely not bad for a man born in January 1911!'

'I feel bad now, I'm just thinking about Queenie. I was never unfaithful to her, you know. Not in all the years I was away. I had the chance, but it never really crossed my mind. Doing…' He paused and reflected on the past few minutes: 'Making love with you sccms so natural.'

'Things are different today. I don't make a habit of sleeping around but it did seem the right thing to do. Still I don't suppose you had much chance in those days. Especially in the prison camp?'

'There was a young bombardier in one of the huts some of the prisoners visited. He was paid in chocolate and tobacco.'

Lizzie made a face.

'But I think Queenie wouldn't have minded after all those years of abstinence.'

'I'll have to get a "morning after pill". Any more love-making and you'll need some condoms. We had better get both in the morning from the pharmacy.'

'Morning after pill?'

'Just in case any little Jacky Fishers get through, after all you haven't had the "snip" have you? A vasectomy that is?'

Fisher said that he hadn't, but said, 'I didn't think of

the possibilities of, as you say a little Jacky Fisher.' He laughed. 'Boy or girl, they could both be called Jacky.'

★

In the morning they called by the pharmacy as planned. The pill and condoms were bought. Lizzie washed the medication down with a small bottle of water purchased in the same shop. She discreetly passed the packets of sheaths to Fisher who stood and openly examined the packaging. Lizzie shook her head in disbelief and hissed at him.

As promised they threw a house warming. Alan and Jack bought Hattie. Neither of Jack's children were available as Suzanne had taken them on holiday to the West Indies. Alan was accompanied by his girlfriend, Helen. The cover story was the same for the neighbours. Fisher had recently left the Army and he and Lizzie were settling into Civvy Street. Helen was told he was a friend of Jack's from his football years.

As soon as they could be out of earshot of the party, as Alan fought vainly through smoke and flames not to incinerate the food, Jack told his grandfather that the satellite channel would be holding a "coming out" programme. To clear the air as Jack told Fisher.

'It will be on our current affairs programme. It goes out from ten until eleven in the morning, weekdays.'

'Bit like a debutante,' Fisher said.

'Wasn't thinking about that sort, but yes you could say that,' Elland replied. 'We are going to have the guys who you turned upon in France, Captain Beckman and Dr Singh.' He paused. 'Our mum, but not Gran, as she's definitely not well. Oh and me and Alan.'

'So all the people who I've met in this world.'

'Two flies in the ointment are Jock Wolf for one, you remember him? But the biggest fly of all, the host is a disagreeable the little snot who could rub the Pope himself up the wrong way. Eamonn Killare. He's been attacked, physically, live on air by footballers, pop singers even the heavyweight champion of the world. He's had politicians threatening him with slander. God only knows why, but the great British public love him.'

'Do we have to go on this programme if it's that bad?'

'You'll walk it, Jacky – from what you've told me about Dieppe and the training camp, plus the events at, where was it now, Stettin? You'll breeze it, plus as I'm acting as your agent I've secured a big payday from my bosses. As you know I've got enough money and this will set you up for life.'

'Will Queenie and Hattie benefit?'

'Our mum has me and Alan to see to her needs. She was a good mum to us both, as was our dad. Gran is cared for by the council in the old folks' home. Ten times the payment wouldn't give Gran a better life, wouldn't bring back her mind. Trust me, Jacky.'

Helen sidled over and spoke to Fisher. 'Alan tells me you've been in the Army. Did you go anywhere interesting?'

Fisher felt a slight panic with the question. 'The usual places, you know.'

'Like?'

'Just the usual. Why do you ask?'

'What did you do?'

Fisher felt on firmer ground. 'Tank driving instructor.'

'What sort?'

'All types.'

Alan rescued him. 'You two getting to know each other?'

'He'd make a good secret agent,' Helen laughed, 'he didn't give much away.'

Harriet joined them. 'We need to make a move now, Jack wants to get back for the dog, as Suzanne and the girls are away.'

★

At the end of the evening and as Jacky and Lizzie waved them away. Jack Elland powered the piano-black Range Rover away up the hill of the anonymous suburban estate. They watched the tail lights as they disappeared from sight.

Jacky took her in his arms as she turned from closing the door. 'Lizzie, when this is over, you know the TV programme and all, can we carry on?'

'What about Victoria?'

Fisher looked pensively at her. 'Yes, Queenie, you're right. Oh I don't know!' He sank back on the sofa. He held his head in his hands. 'It's all so confusing. Here am I a man from the past with,' he looked up at Lizzie, 'a lovely girl from the present. I think I'm falling in love with you Lizzie. Sure I still love Queenie, but it's not the same.'

'Jacky, we've only been together a few weeks. I really like you but—' She paused thinking for a moment, so as to cause no pain. 'I've got my job to do, that was the reason I broke up with my former partner and I'm sometimes away for a week or more. I need to pay my rent.'

'The money I'm getting from the Army and the television station will see us through I know it will. Plus Jack has said he'll buy me, or us, a house. He's a multi-millionaire after all.'

'I'm not a kept woman I'm afraid, Jacky.'

'You won't be. You could transfer to the local police.'

'Be a bloody Plod!' she exploded.

'Is that bad?'

'Giving talks to primary school kids, instead of chasing down bad lads with a Glock in my hand.'

'From what you said, you know about your accident, you were only a glorified nurse maid.'

She looked at him with mock disapproval and flung her arms around his neck. She kissed him deeply and whispered in his ear. 'If I put my nurse maid's outfit on, will you make love to me?'

Chapter Fifteen

All will be revealed

There was a heavy dew on both the grass and cars as Jack steered the black Range Rover to a halt outside the house in Swanley.

Lizzie and Jacky, prompted by a phone call, were waiting outside and walked to the car. She took Fisher's hand and squeezed it tightly.

'You'll be OK, just be yourself.'

He smiled at her: 'I suppose you're right, c'mon let's get it over with.'

Jack Elland greeted his grandfather as the pair climbed into the car: 'All OK, Jacky?'

Lizzie answered for him: 'Just a bit nervy, you know, don't you? I bet it was the same the first time you went on television. My dad used to watch you when you played for Newcastle. Did you know that?'

'Were you a fan, in the day, that is?'

She laughed out loud, 'I'm too young!'

Jack shook his head in mock disbelief.

They set off to London and made good time through

surprisingly light traffic. Fisher recognised the buildings when they arrived at the satellite television headquarters. The gates were opened by a uniformed security guard and Jack Elland parked the car.

They were checked in by security and given photographic passes. It reminded Fisher of the barracks in Gillingham. They were allowed into the foyer after passing through an electronic security scanner and on to the elevators. They were whisked to the top floor where the studios were. As the lift doors opened Fisher was surprised to see three Waffen SS troopers, in full uniform sitting on a large royal blue sofa. They looked so foreign in this High-Tec building Fisher thought.

These men were in the company of an equal number of women. The three re-enactment soldiers stood and walked towards Jack, Lizzie and Fisher.

'Jacky! You're a sight for sore eyes, old son,' enthused Dave Benson as he vigorously shook Fisher's hand.

'Likewise,' Fisher replied; he turned to Lizzie and his grandson. 'This is Lizzie, she's my...'

Lizzie cut in. 'Close friend. I'm Jacky's...let's say minder. Jacky,' she touched his arm lightly, 'I've got a bit to do with my work here. One of my colleagues I need to speak to. I'll be in the studio for the show though. Don't let him get to you. Promise?'

'Lizzie, please stay, I need you here.' She nodded her agreement as Jack Elland stepped forward. He introduced himself.

'I'm Jacky's grandson, you may recognise me.'

The three were in shocked awe at the millionaire footballer's presence.

'Crikey, Jacky, you've fallen on your feet in this world,' Phillip Tasker stated.

Jacky smiled and but then stiffened to attention. 'Jawohl Herr Leutnant!' He burst out laughing.

As the laughter subsided Jim Read indicated the three women. 'These are our wives. He named them in turn leaving his own till last. The names went over Fisher's head and were instantly forgotten.

A young woman emerged from a side door. 'Mr Elland, would you bring your party through, please?'

Fisher followed her lead and the group crowded into a conference room. There was the smell of coffee and on a table a plate of chocolate biscuits. The items that grabbed Jacky Fisher's attention was his uniform, belt and MP40. They were lying on a table adjacent to the coffee pots.

The research assistant spoke. 'The producer would like you to put these clothes on when we do the interview. We want you to bring the—' she paused, looking at the machine pistol '—the gun too.' She looked at Jack Elland and dropped her eyes. 'It comes as part of the deal I'm afraid.' She looked again at Fisher: 'There's a changing room there.' She nodded towards a door. 'Mr Killare wants to meet you all before the show for a briefing.' She left the room, her face glowing pink.

'Poor little love!' Lizzie said. 'I thought she'd melt. Do you have that effect on women, Jack Elland?'

'I've never seen that one. Eamonn Killare's production team are an entirely different section to the football.'

Fisher picked up the uniform. His helmet was there, but Benson stepped forward handing him, a dark green forage cap identical to his own.

'No need for that, trooper.' He tapped Fisher's helmet, 'It's a bit OTT after all. I see you've got your dagger.' He pointed to Fisher's belt. 'I'm still jealous of your MP40 you know!'

Fisher picked up the machine pistol and handed it over. 'I don't suppose they will, but if I get to keep it, I'll give it to you! I'm done with war and killing.' He turned to the uniformed re-enactors, 'I was there, boys. I saw hundreds killed on the beach in Dieppe, trod on the guts of my mates, having seen them ripped apart. Trust me there's nothing good about it. But I know you lads have a passion and that's good.' He gathered up the uniform and turned to Lizzie. 'I'll get this lot on.' He took his machine pistol from Benson and passed it to her. He left the room.

Chapter Sixteen

Welcome Home, Jacky Fisher

Eamonn Killare joined the group. They were on the set of the show. There was an auditorium, but the seats were as yet unoccupied.

'My producer has told you the plan? We are doing a "This is your life" type exposé,' he sniggered, eyeing Fisher, 'you know the sort of thing?'

Fisher shook his head. The effeminate man was getting to him already. Even the smell of the interviewer's cologne affronted him. Before he could answer Lizzie said, 'I'll tell him.'

Killare's bright eyes bored into Fisher's. 'It's only the most famous fecking programme that there's ever been. Everyone's heard of it for the love of God. Where's he been? Oh, of course all the fecking bollocks we're going to hear. Time fecking travel!' He peered, it seemed, through Fisher's soul. 'Fecking time travel. Load of bollocks if you ask me.'

Killare minced off followed by his young woman assistant. Fisher could hear his piercing Irish brogue as Lizzie took him by the arm.

'Don't let him get to you. It's his job. This show is what we call a "dish the dirt" programme. All the commercial channels have one each morning. They are all tripe hounds.'

'He's a nasty piece of work that's for sure. Why does he wear perfume?'

Lizzie gripped his arm and whispered, 'He's gay. Homosexual.'

'He wants everyone to know?'

She nodded her affirmation.

Fisher remembered the young soldier at the camp. That was an open secret he knew.

*

Jacky Fisher stood with an assistant studio manager, he had told Fisher his name was Mike. He gripped Fisher's arm and listened intently through an earpiece.

'Get ready, and when I tell you, go to Eamonn, shake his hand and sit in the chair to the left of him, like I told you earlier.'

Fisher felt sweat course down his muscular spine. The strap of the MP40 was heavy on his shoulder. He wondered why they had insisted he carried it. The coarse material of the clothing made his skin itch. He realised, after wearing modern clothes, how heavy this Waffen SS uniform was. His belt, although devoid of the box magazines in their pouch, was heavy too.

Benson had been correct regarding the dagger. Earlier he had slid it from its scabbard and examined it. Razor-sharp, just how it should be. If a trooper was out of ammunition his dagger or bayonet would always be there for him. He looked up and saw Eamonn Killare as he danced from the other side of the stage. The applause from the audience, who, having been stirred up by another studio manager, rose to a crescendo.

'HELLO, HELLO! HELLO!' The show's host called as he danced onto the stage. He bowed to the studio audience and turned towards his chair. Two cameramen pushed their apparatus towards him following his footsteps. Fisher looked at a monitor near him, Killare's face in close-up was already bathed in sweat.

'Ladies and gentlemen, viewers, friends. Today I have for you, and, I'd like to see your reaction to reports that a man claims he has successfully travelled in time. He's not come back in time, like the "Terminator". No. He's not a robot come to kill us all,' Killare looked into the nearest camera, 'thank the Lord. He claims, and the authorities tell us they think he's genuine. But I ask you to judge,' he paused to snigger at the same camera, 'if this is just a load of old tosh. So let me introduce without further ado, Mr Jacky Fisher, the man who claims to have come from the past.'

Mike released Fisher's arm and pushed him gently. 'Go, go!' he hissed.

Fisher stumbled towards Killare the MP40 banging against his leg. He felt awkward under the heat of the studio lights dressed in his uniform. The host stood offering his hand. Fisher took it, noting the soft sweaty texture of the man's skin.

'Jacky Fisher, you are most welcome. I tell you what viewers, with this bloody great gun here, I'd better watch myself.' He sank back on his chair, motioning his visitor to sit by him. 'I've told the viewers and studio audience that you claim to have come from the past.'

Fisher affirmed this fact. He went to speak but Killare held up his hand to silence him.

'I'd like to bring on three men who CLAIM, yes, claim, viewers, that you appeared out of thin air.' He looked into the camera and reiterated, 'Thin air, viewers!' He sniggered again. 'Without more ado, please welcome Phillip Tasker, Jim Read and Dave Benson! They are from a German army re-enactment group. These guys dress up and run around playing soldiers.' The audience tittered.

The three uniformed re-enactors filed on. They shook hands with Killare and Jacky, taking seats alongside Fisher.

Killare spoke first to Tasker. 'I'm told you and your friends here like to dress up as,' he consulted his notes, 'to look like Wuffen SS?'

'It's pronounced Vaffen, the "W" is "V",' Tasker tried to explain.

'Oh sure, oh you don't say,' Killare said. 'You still dress up as soldiers. I mean Ireland was sensible enough to stay out of Britain's little war, well the second one anyway. So we don't need to play at war. We like the finer things in life. Guinness for one. Do you agree?'

Killare once again cut off any reply. Fisher had seen Captain Beckman and Dr Singh waiting to come on the set. The Irish host called them on and greeted them. They in turn shook hands with Fisher and the re-enactors. They sat to Killare's right. He turned to them.

'Captain Beckman and Dr Singh, I understand Mr Fisher here was turned in to you. What made you sure that he was genuine?'

Singh began to speak, 'It was his picture from the Army…'

'We have that here…' Killare cut the Asian doctor dead.

The studio monitor changed to a monochrome image of Fisher.

'You're saying this is this man.' He motioned to Fisher and sniggered again. 'It was supposed to have been taken before the war. Also Captain Beckman, we've been doing so digging. It turns out your grandfather was a Nazi!'

'He was a mechanic in the Army.'

Killare sniggered once again and a camera caught his close-up: 'Now that would be the German army? The Nazi army!'

'He was a soldier, working under orders.'

'Oh yeah, I think that's what they *all* said. We were under orders. Under orders if you please.' A camera zoomed in on him as he spat the words out.

Before Beckman could answer, Killare cut him off. 'We are running short on time as we have a surprise visitor coming to the studio.' He touched his earpiece, 'I'm told Mr Fisher, that tradition decrees those prisoners of war, soldiers, airmen or sailors who escaped from captivity in Nazi-held Europe would meet the Prime Minister; at the time of course it was Mr Winston Churchill.

Fisher looked up as Eamonn Killare stood. The host began clapping. The audience too were on their feet. Fisher recognised the slightly built woman in her early forties as she walked on to the set. She had two well-built men with her, he guessed they were her security detail.

'Ladies and Gentlemen, viewers at home, I give you the British Prime Minster.' The clapping from the crowd increased with people whooping and cheering. The noise drowned out the effeminate Irishman's voice: 'Clare Martin!'

Fisher stood; he saw Lizzie approaching with the Prime Minister's entourage. She was deep in conversation with one of the security personnel, a dark-haired man. Fisher was aware of Clare Martin walking to him. She smiled and held out her hand. 'It's been a long time getting you home, Jacky. On behalf of the British people, Welcome Home, Jacky Fisher.'

Fisher's feet felt as he were glued to the spot. Cold sweat ran from his forehead and stung his eyes. He thought of the dental surgery and the violent dreams. Lizzie looked over at him and smiled. He felt a hand on his back. It was Eamonn Killare. 'What are you waiting for? Shake the Prime Minister's hand, yer bloody fool.' He pushed Fisher forward. 'This is my show, don't fuck it up!' Fisher heard him hiss.

Fisher reached down to his belt and snatched the dagger from its scabbard. He turned on the ball of his foot and drove the blade under Killare's chin, pinning his tongue to the roof of his mouth, the blade piercing the man's brain – in the way he had practised on the Russian prisoners, stilling the man's filthy scornful words. The warm life blood gushed as Fisher withdrew the knife. He felt the weight of the talk show host falling against him as the life was snatched from him. As he pulled the blade out, he turned to Clare Martin. He was confronted by Lizzie standing between him and the Prime Minister.

'Don't do it, Jacky, you don't need to. Put the blade down!'

Fisher saw that Clare Martin was now surrounded by her bodyguards. Summoning his strength, he pushed past Lizzie. He saw the fear in the Prime Minister's face. He couldn't understand why though. Jack Elland called to him, and he paused for a second, looking into his grandson's eyes.

'Jacky, what are you doing?' Elland demanded.

More bodyguards had surrounded Clare Martin now, they had appeared from behind the set, and were ushering her away.

One man was holding an object in his hand, pointing it at Fisher. 'Look at me, Mr Fisher. Put the knife down, put it down, man!' He called. 'I won't hesitate to fire, put it down!'

Several police officers had drawn their guns. Fisher looked down at his MP40. A full magazine of 9mm shells would scythe this stage of life. Even though there was no ammunition, he snatched at the strap pulling the machine pistol into the firing position.

The officer with the Taser didn't shout another warning. Fisher heard the crack of the gas cartridge and raised the Schmeisser to protect his body. The barbed dart ricocheted from the gun and struck Fisher's throat. His body went rigid and he crashed to the floor.

Lizzie reached him first. 'Oh God, Jacky, what were you thinking?' She felt for a pulse and found none. 'Someone call an ambulance!' Jack Elland helped Lizzie roll Fisher on to his back and together they tried to resuscitate the prone figure. It was to no avail.

Chapter Seventeen

Was it a dream?

It was damp and almost completely dark as Fisher regained consciousness. The odour from the explosion was still fresh in his lungs.

His senses were numbed and the red hue before his eyes accentuated the banging in his brain from the concussive blast and the bright flash of the bomb. This made his head swim as he tried to stand. His eyes fought vainly to adjust to the gloom, the damp sense in his nose imbibed into his brain.

He stayed kneeling for a few seconds. He thought of Hattie, Queenie, Jack and Alan Elland. Lizzie the house in Swanley, the television studios, the woman Prime Minister. Was it, could it have been a dream? He looked at his left wrist in the darkness and pressed the button on the watch. He squinted at the LCD readout, the time still moved relentlessly on. He looked at the date 8-8-1943.

As his eyes adjusted he could see part of Peters' torso had come down the shell hoist. He stood and looked along the main gallery. To his surprise there was a large crack in the reinforced concrete. It had been torn apart like wet cardboard. It was obvious the bunker was finished as a structure. The floor was at an unusual angle too. As he progressed along the passage he was aware the magazine door had been forced open by the blast, the neatly stacked shells for the 88s and the flak batteries cascading from their racks onto the concrete floor.

★

Half a mile away and closing fast, 2nd Lieutenant Tom Filmer saw the "bunker buster" hit the concrete control and command centre fair and square. The smoke was clearing and he thought of the men who manned this vital hub. His boss Major Mclaren soared off towards the waiting P51 Mustang escorts that were covering the operation from high above.

Now Filmer thought, it was his turn – his job, as it had been described in the days of training back in the deserts of Nevada. The bunker buster had the a "tin opener" effect on these concrete monoliths, so that he, Tom Filmer, could deliver one of the new, so called "oil bombs". He had seen the destructive power of both types of ordinance and he sure felt sorry for the guys on the receiving end.

The Lockheed Lightning was some piece of kit. A single-seater with twin turbo-charged engines, contra-rotating, so as to try and eliminate the torque-pull that all aircraft suffered from on take-off and landing. Sure it could not out-fly an FW190, it was maybe not even matched against the Messerschmitt 109. But, boy, if some square-head got between him and his six .50 machine guns he could make a mess of them.

Tom held the plane steady and, using his bomb sight, dropped the lethal light-case canister. He imagined it as he had seen in training films, rolling through the air before splitting open, the pre-heated petro-magnesium mixture burning, running rivers of fire, and seeking out stored ammunition and gasoline.

He opened the throttles wide, pushing past the "emergency boost seals". He needed to put distance between the target and damn quick too. He felt the concussive blast as he accelerated away. Pulling the fighter-bomber to the right, he witnessed the total destruction of the bunker as giant slabs of reinforced concrete were thrown skywards as the magazine exploded.

He looked for his Mustang escorts and his boss Major Mclaren.

'Job done!' Tom Filmer heard through his headphones from one of the escorts above. He checked his compass and after joining up with the others they all set a course for home. The bunker burned for several days, but after a raid of such a magnitude the local fire fighters had more important tasks extinguishing fires in the war production factories and surrounding workers' houses.

Epilogue

Jacky Fisher was buried in the same grave as Queenie, who passed away two days after him. The service was in the local cemetery close to his old home in Chelmsford Essex. It was a quiet affair; Lizzie, Major Willis, Captain Planer, Jack and Alan Elland plus their close families. The members of the re-enactment group came along. Fisher's uniform including the much prized MP40 machine-pistol and the SS dagger were donated by his grandsons to a war museum, where a display was mounted featuring the little known activities of the "British Free Corps", a detachment in the Wehrmacht, the war-time German Army.

Lizzie was relieved that "no little Jacky Fishers" got past the contraceptive pill and resumed her career in the Close Protection Squad. Jack returned to broadcasting and Alan to selling cars.

The site of the anti-aircraft bunkers above the modern Polish town of Szczecin is overgrown. The whole area is fenced off with signs warning of unexploded ordnance. The concrete is mainly covered in green algae and exposed re-enforcing is red with rust. Anyone foolish enough to venture into the crushed and mangled bunker might discover the bones of a long-lost soldier. Would the melted plastic material of the digital watch survive?

This skeleton, if it were discovered, had a twin buried in an Essex town 1300km away.